The
Unresolved
Past

A Debate
in German
History

The Unresolved Past

A Conference
sponsored by the
Wheatland
Foundation

Chaired and
Introduced by
Ralf Dahrendorf

Edited by
Gina Thomas

A Debate in German History

Weidenfeld and Nicolson
London

Published in association with the
Wheatland Foundation by
George Weidenfeld and Nicolson Ltd
91 Clapham High St
London, SW4 7TA

Typeset, printed and bound by
Butler & Tanner Ltd,
Frome and London

ISBN 0 297 82033 8

Contents

The Unresolved Past
A Debate in German History

A Wheatland Foundation Conference
September 1987

Ann Getty, President of the Wheatland Foundation
Lord Weidenfeld, Chairman of the Wheatland Foundation

The conference was chaired by Professor Sir Ralf Dahrendorf, Warden of St Antony's College, Oxford.

Participants
Lord Annan, former Vice-Chancellor, University of London.
Sir Isaiah Berlin, Fellow of All Souls College and former President of Wolfson College, Oxford.
Robert Conquest, Senior Research Fellow, Hoover Institute, Stanford University.
Gordon Craig, J. E. Wallace Sterling Professor of Humanities (Emeritus), Stanford University.
Lord Dacre, (Hugh Trevor-Roper) former Regius Professor of History, Oxford.
Samuel Ettinger, Professor of Jewish History, Hebrew University of Jerusalem.
Joachim Fest, Publisher, *Frankfurter Allgemeine Zeitung.*
Saul Friedlander, Professor of History, Tel Aviv University.
Felix Gilbert, Emeritus Professor, Princeton University.
Carol Gluck, Sansom Professor of Japanese History, Colombia University.
Sir Nicholas Henderson, former British Ambassador to Washington, Paris and Bonn.
Eberhard Jäckel, Professor of Modern History, Universität Stuttgart.
Harold James, Assistant Professor of History, Princeton University.
Jürgen Kocka, Professor of Modern History, Freie Universität Berlin.

Charles Maier, Professor of European History, Harvard University.

Christian Meier, Professor of Ancient History, Universität München.

Hans Mommsen, Professor of Modern History, Ruhr-Universität Bochum.

Wolfgang Mommsen, Professor of Modern History, Universität Düsseldorf.

Julius Schoeps, Professor of Political Science at Duisburg University, Director of the Saloman-Ludwig Steinheim Institute for German-Jewish History.

Hagen Schulze, Professor of Modern History, Universität der Bundeswehr München.

Fritz Stern, Seth Low Professor of Modern History, Columbia University.

Norman Stone, Professor of Modern History, Worcester College, Oxford.

Michael Stürmer, Stiftung Wissenschaft und Politik, Ebenhausen.

Introduction
The Unresolved Past

When the Wheatland Foundation invited me to chair a conference on the German *Historikerstreit*, I wondered whether the issue was still sufficiently alive to warrant yet another meeting. I was wrong. It is true that by then the historians' dispute had been going on, mostly in the columns of two German newspapers, the *Frankfurter Allgemeine Zeitung* and *Die Zeit*, for more than a year. Given the pace of modern life, the dispute itself was beginning to become history; it was as much the subject of articles as were the issues at stake with publishers competing for collected editions of the various contributions. The difficulties they met with should have warned me. Such were the animosities roused by the dispute that some of the participants refused to have their pieces published in the same volume as those of their opponents. Similar difficulties arose over invitations to the Wheatland Conference. Many months later the ripples even reached these shores when Ernst Nolte, one of the originators of the debate, was again 'disinvited', this time not from a public appearance in Frankfurt but from lecturing at an Oxford college.

At the end of the Wheatland Conference a British participant known for his ironical and often caustic comments, remarked that the meeting had told him as much about German historians as about German history. He meant, of course, that he had learned little about past events and a great deal about the tone and style adopted by those who make it their profession to understand history in the pursuit of their task. It is indeed hard to avoid the impression that the fire generated by the dispute bears no relation to the light which it sheds on history. There is another way of putting this observation: it is not altogether easy to tell what exactly the *Historikerstreit* was about.

The reader of this transcript will see that, as chairman, I put this question to the participants once or twice during the conference without however eliciting a clear answer. Let me therefore venture some kind of answer myself. Without doubt, the dispute was sparked off by statements about Auschwitz. When Saul Friedlander left a party in Berlin in disgust, or when the organizers of the Römerberg-Gespräche in Frankfurt decided to cancel a lecture which they themselves had commissioned, the immediate reason lay in an assessment of Auschwitz which was deemed unacceptable. In both cases it was Ernst Nolte's assessment. It is important to state at the outset that Ernst Nolte is a philosopher-historian of considerable repute who is taken seriously both at home and abroad. He is not involved in anti-democratic activities, nor does he in any way attempt to justify these wherever they occur. Rather, Nolte is trying to establish a new context in which to judge the incomprehensible crimes of the Nazi regime, and he finds this context in the 'Asiatic mode of killing', in Bolshevism. He argues that Hitler and his henchmen not only did something which Stalin had done before them, but that the National Socialists actually borrowed their plans to eradicate the Jews from the Soviet Union. In concrete terms which must be puzzling to many historians, Nolte restated his thesis 'that in the gulag archipelago lay the origins of Auschwitz; and that anti-Bolshevism was a far more compelling motive for Hitler than anti-Semitism' (in an article in the London *Independent* on 5 November 1988).

Characteristically, Nolte was not immediately asked to present the evidence for his claim. Instead, his interpretation was questioned. From the outset, evidence played a minor part in the dispute, for the *Historikerstreit* was about interpretation, not about history. Two successive Presidents of the German Historical Association, Wolfgang Mommsen and Christian Meier – both participants of the Wheatland Conference – held their own divergent interpretations against Nolte's and they did so in no uncertain terms. In an article published alongside Nolte's in the *Independent*, Mommsen speaks of Nolte's 'half-truths' and says, 'Whereas they add little to historical knowledge, they will be seen by all those who have learned nothing from the past as justification for their view that National Socialism was not so bad after all.'

This, it will be remembered, was not a dispute between men who were personally involved in Nazi Germany, nor was it one between a new generation trying to come to terms with the immediate past of its country. The historians' dispute broke out forty years after the end of the war. One is almost tempted to add

that it was a part of those curious fortieth anniversary 'celebrations' which have become fashionable ever since the leaders
of the wartime allies assembled on Omaha Beach to commemorate
the Normandy invasion. Why the past should have caught up
with the present after forty, rather than twenty-five, or fifty years
is the subject of much speculation. Why was Mr Waldheim an
undisputed Foreign Minister of his country and twice appointed
Secretary General of the United Nations, only to find the world
turning against him forty years after the war when he stood for
the Presidency of Austria?

The Wheatland Conference failed to give an answer to this
question. However, in Germany's case there are perhaps reasons
which lend a certain plausibility to the rediscovery of history.
Take the laying of wreaths at Bitburg cemetery by Chancellor
Kohl and President Reagan in 1985, a site chosen although it
contained the war graves of German soldiers, some of whom had
been members of the Waffen-SS. Chancellor Kohl felt that the
time had come to bury the past. He, who by 'the grace of late
birth', as he put it on his visit to Israel, did not feel involved in
the crimes of the Nazis, wanted to reconcile Germany with its
past and, through the symbolic presence of the President of the
United States, involve Germany's new-found allies in the process.
Kohl somehow sought to link the whole of Germany, past and
present, with the new role of the Federal Republic in the 1980s.
He thought the time was ripe for such a venture. Clearly, it did
not work. As he could have learned from his own President,
Richard von Weizsäcker, the past will not pass away so easily.

Why did Chancellor Kohl want to do such a thing? One can
only guess, and to some extent extrapolate. One interpretation of
Bitburg is, that it was intended to free Germany of all remaining
shackles and thereby enable it to establish an identity like other
nations whilst opening up opportunities for a more independent
foreign policy. Is it mere accident that Bitburg coincided with a
tentative, yet unmistakable revival of ideas of *Mitteleuropa*, and a
debate about Germany's role between the two powers rather than
on one side of the divide? French fears of a Germany drifting away
from its European and Western commitments are undoubtedly
exaggerated. Yet many wondered at the time what to make of
opinion polls which not only showed that Gorbachev was more
popular in the Federal Republic than Reagan, but also that
Germans trusted Soviet policy more than they trusted the United
States of America. This is not the place to explore such questions

in depth. However, they point to real developments which played some part in the passions generated by the *Historikerstreit*. For the debate was essentially political. History was manipulated to make contemporary points. Even Auschwitz was not the real subject of the dispute, but an instrument in an interpretation of history which served contemporary purposes.

Nolte's first opponent, Jürgen Habermas, saw this clearly. (Though invited, neither Habermas nor Nolte took part in the Wheatland Conference, but their presence was felt throughout.) Being not only a man of the political left, but a Hegelian and the contemporary executor of the Frankfurt School of critical theory, Habermas has never been an unquestioning defender of the Federal Republic of Germany, its leaders and its international alliances. But the attempt to establish a continuous strand of German history across Auschwitz with a view to constructing a German identity unburdened by the damage done in the past, provoked him to state a position which came as a surprise to some. When the chips are down, Habermas belongs to the West. The 'constitutional patriotism' which he advocated in his original attack on Nolte and several other authors is part of the service rendered by his generation to Germany, and that is to make the Federal Republic an unambiguous part of the enlightened Western tradition of thinking and institutional formation. Within this tradition, Auschwitz is an aberration which cannot be explained away by any stretch of historical interpretation.

The *Historikerstreit* is a very German phenomenon. It boiled up at a stage when, for the first time, a generation of leaders felt free to place the country in a historical and political context defined by them rather than by the circumstances of 1945. Small wonder that this opportunity raised conflicting views, old and new passions, and some sleeping dogs. It was probably an accident that historians and their interpretations of Auschwitz became the vehicle of public debate. One may even ask whether it was a happy accident. It did not help the historical profession or raise its standing, nor did it result in a clear definition of the issue. But it is no use crying over spilt milk. In any case, the dispute was sufficiently public to have allowed many non-historians to express their views. Why hold a conference in England about a dispute which is as German as these comments imply? Some of the participants of the Wheatland Conference may have asked themselves that question. The non-Germans felt a little like voyeurs at times, and the Germans tried to concentrate on matters of more general interest rather than continue their 'domestic' debate. But then, domestic German affairs have long been of more than academic interest for the rest of Europe and beyond. This applies particularly to Germany's history in the twentieth century and its place in tomorrow's world and has become all the more pertinent in the light of recent developments in Eastern Europe.

Beyond the obvious ramifications of German problems, there are at least two wider issues which arose out of the *Historikerstreit*, and which were the subject of the Wheatland Conference. One of these issues concerned the way in which traumatic events of the past should be dealt with. The question of whether Auschwitz can and should be compared to other experiences of genocide is a red herring. Comparison is as inevitable as it is inadequate when it comes to explanation. But it is important to find out how countries, peoples, or those who speak and write in and for them, deal with events in their history which defy all normal categories of analysis. The Soviet Union is going through a period of soul-searching, which appears at times to leave no stone unturned. Whilst official spokesmen still try to draw a line between the unacceptable face of Stalin and the acceptable one of Lenin, some authors have begun to cross even this line, so that no phase of the history of Communist Russia remains unturned.

In Japan the analogous process is less public, or at any rate less apparent to Western eyes; but some of the agonies of Japan's attempt to come to terms with its history were brought to light by the slow death of Emperor Hirohito. It seemed appropriate therefore to ask Robert Conquest and Carol Gluck to give the Wheatland Conference the benefit of their knowledge of these experiences. They illustrated, as did the German dispute, that history can be of passionate importance in contemporary debates. Purists may not like this; they may pursue the old mirage of what actually happened; but it is a mirage. The past comes to life by the way in which it relates to the present and to plans for the future. The relationship is complex. It is, in fact, the other issue on the agenda of the Conference on which this volume reports.

Perhaps this particular gathering demonstrated rather than discussed the uses of history. The recent book by Richard Neustadt and Ernest May, *Thinking in Time*, has explored 'the uses of history for decision-makers' by reference to particular incidents in recent American history. Nothing sums up the gist of this book better than Robert Kennedy's citation of an older saying during the Cuban missile crisis, 'Good judgement is usually the result of experience. And experience is frequently the result of bad judgement.' The quotation is apposite in the context of this conference. Ultimately, it was a conference on how to avoid some of the great crimes of the past. In order to do so, we have to understand not only how they came about, but also how people came to terms with them, why they acquiesced at the time and how they coped when they discovered what had happened. This is not a subject which leads to clear and unambiguous conclusions.

As one reads the transcript of the Wheatland Conference one cannot fail to be aware of how much remains unresolved. Thus the title of the conference, and of this book, is as pertinent at the end as it was at the beginning; it is about the unresolved past. Although the events in Eastern Europe have rendered the *Historikerstreit* itself obsolete, it serves as an illustration of the way in which German historians allowed political and ideological considerations to encroach on their assessment of the past. In the end, the British participant who felt he had learnt as much about German historians as about German history at the conference hit the nail on the head. The transcript of the Wheatland Conference provides an insight into the German psyche and as such it has documentary value.

Ralf Dahrendorf

The conference opened with two introductory papers dealing with issues raised by the *Historikerstreit*.

CHARLES MAIER: I have to declare a personal interest in this debate. My first exposure to Germany was as a high school exchange student in the summer of 1955. Coming from a German-Jewish background, I had naturally thought about the questions which have now been raised by the historians' debate. I have taught in Germany, I have colleagues in Germany, many of whom are involved in this debate and I am preparing a book on it.*

I want to concentrate on what I think the long-term issues are for historians and for historiography. I have selected three issues. One is historical comparison. When is comparison legitimate, when is it tendentious? Another issue involves the question of identity. What can historians say about national identity? Is it defined historically? The third question concerns the nature of historical rhetoric and discourse: Has this debate exceeded the bounds of what should be acceptable discourse among historians, and if so, what should these bounds be?

Let me say a few things regarding the issue of timing. Why did this controversy arise now? One reason is contingency, the dates of the wartime anniversaries. Ralf Dahrendorf mentioned D-Day and Bitburg. These celebrations enabled those who participated in the events and younger generations to experience a certain conjunction of perspectives. This was probably one of the few occasions when the post-war generation could be fully involved and question their elders about the past. Secondly, there is what has been labelled the *Tendenzwende*, the conservative turn of the tide. We have experienced a change in political temperament and political discussion in many different areas. This also has consequences for the social sciences.

There has been a general turn toward what one might call subjectivity in history and the social sciences, a dissatisfaction with the great behavioural projects of the 1950s, with socio-economic, or neo-Marxist approaches. There has been a move away from the concept that history can be reduced to a social science, away from quantifying social theory and back to the idea of what the Germans would call a *verstehende Geisteswissenschaft*, that is an approach to knowledge through intuitive under-

---

*Published as *The Unmasterable Past: History, Holocaust and German National Identity* (Cambridge, Mass., 1988).

standing, a renewed acceptance of 'historicist' efforts at empathy or perhaps more rigorously, through the use of ideal types. There has been a recovery of anthropological methods, of interpretive anthropology. There is clearly a relationship, although it has not always been perceived by the participants, between the growth of 'everyday' history, *Alltagsgeschichte*, and the type of 'historicization' which has been demanded both by historians of the left and the right in Germany. There has been a polarization of figures like Martin Broszat on the one hand and the more conservative spokesmen on the right. The demand for historicization in the German profession seems to be part of a general demand for neo-historicism and a growth in subjectivity.

The fascination with memory has also played its part. This is no accident. Many memoirs have come out recently; here I will mention only Saul Friedlander's eloquent, *When Memory Comes*, which was published a few years ago. The recovery of memory has been one of the most poignant aspects of this debate; that is why it has been so gripping. Let me turn to the three major areas I want to cover: comparison, identity, and rhetoric. In his article 'Vergangenheit, die nicht vergehen will', ('A past that will not pass away') which the *Frankfurter Allgemeine Zeitung* published in spring 1986, Ernst Nolte asserted that one could not understand the Final Solution without also understanding the experience of Soviet terror. He felt that the repression attendent upon the civil war and the Stalinist purges of the 1930s might have served as a direct model for Hitler. He argued that it was incumbent upon historians to compare the Soviet and Nazi experiences and that in fact the German Final Solution was in some sense a consequence of the Soviet terror, which he described as a precedent for the Holocaust. In a subsequent article Joachim Fest threw in other genocides, but they were less essential to the argument. The Armenian or the Cambodian massacres would also attenuate the specialness of the Holocaust, but for Nolte it was clearly a Russo-German (or Soviet-National Socialist) linkage that was crucial.

By and large Joachim Fest supported Nolte's right to bracket these two experiences. He also apparently endorsed Nolte's argument that Hitler might well have been prompted by the Soviet precedent; at the least, it was a legitimate speculation. I must confess that I was very disturbed by the two articles by Professor Nolte. I think that they extended the bounds of acceptable political rhetoric within the Federal Republic. When the question of performing Rainer Fassbinder's play, *Garbage, the City, and Death*,

arose earlier in Frankfurt, Mr Fest argued in the *Fra*
Allgemeine that it would be indecent to stage it. The hist
debate has brought up many of the same issues; none
because the tone seemed more elevated and it was conducted by
academics and intellectuals, Professor Nolte was spared the same
condemnation. The academic style has made legitimate a type of
comparison that had not, I believe, been previously acceptable in
the Federal Republic.

Joachim Fest and others have asked whether those who feel as
I do are not trying to prevent legitimate historical comparison or
to place certain subjects under a taboo. I would say no. Every
question must be addressed, but not all answers have to be
credited. Nolte's contribution was I think, an attempt to propose
answers under the guise of questions. He supposedly asked: was
it not legitimate to compare Nazi and Soviet mass murder? In fact
he implied a particular conclusion should be drawn; that is,
without Stalinism the murder of the Jews would not have been
conceivable or sufficiently motivated. To be sure, his rhetoric
remained tentative. And to be sure, as Professor Nolte has written
elsewhere, without the experience of the Russian Revolution, a
fascist reaction in Western and Central Europe might never have
achieved power. Still, the thrust of the argument was to displace
historical guilt – not by virtue of solid argument but by tentative
hypotheses and hypothetical questions. The subjunctive was used
more frequently in these two articles than in anything I have
encountered since reading Robert Musil's *Man without Qualities*.
The subjunctive is a wonderful tense in German, it allows one to
express all sorts of shadings, but it should not be used to smuggle
in the indicative.

Professor Eberhard Jäckel wrote a very good refutation of
Nolte's comparison in which he pointed out the differences
between the Soviet terror and Hitler's Final Solution. The issue is
not about how many were killed. If Robert Conquest instructs us
correctly, the number of Stalin's victims exceeded Hitler's. Of
course, legitimate comparisons can be sought – one can count
victims, compare judicial proceedings or the lack thereof, ask
about the ideological function of terror, and so on. But reading
Nolte's argument I felt that the unique aspects of the Final Solution
were being trivialized.

Let me recall one image. Those of you who have seen *Shoah*
will remember that Claude Lanzmann relied extensively on the
image of trains. Their recurrence makes a historical point. It

reveals both the planned purposefulness and the European-wide aspirations of Nazi genocide. This was an important aspect of the Final Solution. The regime rounded up people in Westerbork, Saloniki, Warsaw, collected them from all over and brought them then to places where they were to be killed. In many cases they were not even used as labour. The victims were selected by virtue of their group identity. Behaviour was irrelevant.

This sets the Holocaust apart even from a regime which deals with enemies within or in some paranoid way defines almost everybody as enemies, then works them to death or kills them one by one. This is not to say the Final Solution was worse than the Soviet terror; it is just to state that it was different. And diminishing uniqueness could not but have an apologetic effect. For Nolte, the Final Solution and the Nazi role, became just another unfortunate lapse in history, one that finally had to be put in perspective.

Does all this mean that certain historical issues are off limits or taboo, certain versions of events beyond question? Should hesitation about political ramifications mean that historians should not pose real questions, compare dreadful experiences lest they lose their dreadful uniqueness? Not at all. How then do we judge whether a given comparison is justified? Unfortunately I believe that only future research justifies a comparison in scholarly terms. We know whether a comparison is fruitful when another generation uses it, builds on it and makes it a base for further research and conclusions. Comparisons which do not stand this test are captious, arbitrary, fictitious, they lead to dead ends. There is no way of saying definitely at the time it is made that one comparison is fruitful, the other is not. It depends on future work and in part on our own political and subjective stances.

But if comparison must wait for its confirmation, as it were, we can at least say that some comparative statements are inauthentic from the outset. Nolte has relied on questions about language, not about events. He has asked in effect, 'Can we not say that Auschwitz has points of comparison with purges, or derived from the purges?' He is asking less about events than the admissibility of questions and thus can become indignant if admissibility is refused. This is less a historiographical than a rhetorical or moral argument. My feeling is that as such it cannot claim to be a legitimate historical exercise. (However, even if it were a simple declarative proposition, it is possible to show how flawed it is, although I will not labour that argument here.)

What is clear is that German historiography, more than most, has been a battle for control of the relevant comparisons. They constitute political issues as well as historical ones. The situation is reminiscent of Humpty Dumpty's view of language in *Alice in Wonderland*: when I use a word it means what I choose it to mean. Well, a great deal more than words is at stake here.

Secondly, let me take up the question of identity and identification. The question of identification is raised by the procedure that Professor Andreas Hillgruber evoked in his essays concerning the German situation in early 1945, which was published in *Zweierlei Untergang*, ('Two Kinds of Downfall'). I do not attribute any apologetic intention to Hillgruber. He is one of the foremost interpreters of Hitler's strategic and political decision-making processes. In his essay he sought to respond to critics of the German army, who suggested that its defence of the Eastern Front prolonged the horrors of the Nazi regime. Hillgruber responded that the historian had to 'identify' with the perceptions of the Wehrmacht to understand the commitment of soldiers who were defending their country. He dealt with the issue as if he were following a traditional Rankean 'historicist' procedure. I think he was wrong.

I am sorry that Professor Hillgruber is not here, because I do not like to criticize him in his absence, but I think that his appeal to *identification* represented a form of pseudo-historicism. In history either all protagonists deserve the empathy involved in the operation of identification or none of them does. A one-sided identification with the Wehrmacht alone is not a sufficient historiographical procedure. If the historian is going to choose the Wehrmacht, then why not explicate the Army's behaviour as of 1941, why not discuss the shooting of prisoners of war or Communist Party officials, instead of 1945? Can we choose at will where we enter into the historical flux of events to examine and justify the logic of protagonists? The logic of defending East Prussia in 1945 cannot be plucked from the logic of Barbarossa on 22 June 1941.

From identification, one moves to identity: the historian's supposed role in fostering national identity forms a third major strand of this debate. As I read Michael Stürmer's essays, the argument is roughly as follows: West Germans have suffered from a deficit of historical orientation. They are searching for a usable past and the responsible historian must provide it, lest it be left to demagogues or bad historians. History, to use the German expression, involves *Sinnstiftung*, endowment with meaning, endowment with identity.

Michael Stürmer and Hagen Schulze have moreover offered a particular model of identity. Hagen Schulze has written a piece entitled *Wir sind, was wir geworden sind*, ('We are what we have become'). The model put forward is the concept of the *Land der Mitte*, meaning the nation which lies in the middle of Europe and faces powerful neighbours on both sides. This idea of the pressures from without bringing about particular internal developments has been used to explain the German character or the emergence of German identity. It is set against the more socio-economic model of the *Primat der Innenpolitik*, the primacy of home affairs, according to which Germany's policy was largely determined by its internal class stratifications. The latter concept also poses problems, but I do not believe that this model of the *Land der Mitte* adequately summarizes German identity. Poland is also a *Land der Mitte* with equally difficult borders and yet Poland and Germany have radically different histories.

I would like to ask Professor Schulze: Are national identities no more than what their history is? The anthropologist has a different approach, a more structural approach. I do not think the summing-up of national identity can be left to the historian alone, if indeed it can be explained at all. Jürgen Habermas' model of national identity is a difficult one. He speaks of *Verfassungspatriotismus*, meaning literally, constitutional patriotism, a West German identification with a form of international Kantian liberalism and commitment to law and liberty. It is very appealing, very like the eighteenth century concept of a *république des lettres*, but I do not think it is adequate either. Habermas tried to wrestle with the difficulties in his Sonning Prize address given to a Danish audience. In this speech he admitted that he too is committed to the concept of a national identity, and that aspects of this identity must be grounded in a much more psychological, almost Burkeian organic community feeling. It is a complex argument which I cannot adequately recapitulate here. The point is that from Habermas on the left to Michael Stürmer and Hagen Schulze on the other side, not to mention more outright nationalists, there has been a feeling that much of this debate is about national identity and the relationship of history to identity.

I do not think historians should see themselves in the identity business. We cannot provide identity. *Sinnstiftung* is, I feel, beyond us. Michael Stürmer has said the historian must climb a narrow path that is both critical of myth-making and yet looks for meaning. I am not sure it is a feasible path. The concept of identity has been used fuzzily in this debate and obviously we should try to clarify it.

Finally, I would like to raise the question of rhetoric. Thomas Nipperdey, whose work I admire, reproached Habermas for his excessively pointed argumentative style. Habermas' grouping of the three tendencies as one neo-conservative project may have been overdrawn. The question is, however, can the historian be too argumentative? To what extent are we allowed to have a controversy like this? And at what point does it overstep the limits of useful confrontation? I sympathize with Nipperdey's view that history is a fragile craft. On the other hand, the *Historikerstreit* has not primarily been a controversy among historians in their historical texts. This is a controversy in which the participants took to the *Feuilleton*. The existence of this genre in Germany, its non-existence in the Anglo-Saxon world makes the *Historikerstreit* a very different kind of controversy to the one we had for instance over the origins of the Cold War twenty years ago in America.

History is not primarily an adversarial craft although it involves argument and evidence. We are not engaged as lawyers to acquit clients. We are not serving as politicians to win votes. Under normal circumstances we have, perhaps, a commitment to being like French judges, to investigate and try to determine an approximation of the truth. The *Historikerstreit* had its forum outside the history books and academic journals. Personally, I feel indebted to Habermas for having stepped into the controversy as an outsider and for having tried to identify the historiographical trends he saw emerging. It does not mean I hold Habermas free from criticism or that I would endorse this procedure for writing history *ab initio*. But the historiographical ambiance was already highly charged. To say the Left or the Right is more to blame seems to me not very useful. Everyone has approached this controversy with great zest. This has not been without political value. For the first time since the rearmament debate Germans have discussed what it means to be German, what it means to live today with that past and not merely where the borders of Germany should lie (one of the great issues of *Ostpolitik*), or what the nature of the political economy is because Germany has been, for most institutional purposes, a political economy. That is why I have found it one of the most fascinating debates to have taken place in post-war Germany.

CHRISTIAN MEIER: Although I am Chairman of the German Historians' Association, I will try to express my personal opinion. Even if everything else about the *Historikerstreit* is controversial, I think we can all agree that it consists of a series of newspaper articles sparked off by Jürgen Habermas' piece which in turn referred to other publications. One other factor is not contested: none of the authors of articles addressing themselves to this question in any way denies either the fact or the extent of German crimes. Differences only arise as soon as it comes to evaluating these crimes.

It is well known that the debate centered largely around the theory of the singularity of the German crimes. A number of unusual points were made in this context. At first everybody acknowledged this singularity, but later some of the participants tried after all to relativize it. I do not want to comment on that here. Instead I will try to take a detached view.

First of all, it is worth pointing out that although the controversy was on the whole conducted by historians, it met with an unusually strong public response. This was not only because the media had nothing better to focus its attention on at that particular time. A great many people were deeply affected by the matter. This can be deduced from letters written to newspapers, from discussions and lectures which dealt with this question again and again.

In a way the public debate is a war that was waged vicariously. At heart it was about other issues. Though seldom addressed, the real question lurking in the background was: how can a people come to terms with this past? In order to deal with this it is important to establish whether this past is unique or not, how unique it is and whether the crimes can be put on a par with Stalin's, Pol Pot's and other genocides or not. In this context we must ask ourselves: can we be a normal nation, are we stained by this past? This leads to a host of other questions: to what extent are our domestic or foreign policies paralysed by the past or a false perception of the past? It has often been said that we have too little self-assurance because we are marked by obsessive guilt. I cannot agree with this, but it has been an important aspect of the debate. A great deal of politics came into the controversy which also raised the overall question: what are we allowed to do, what can we do with this past weighing us down?

The first thing we have to bear in mind is the specific character of this past. In my opinion the German crimes were unique for reasons which are explained in the Piper volume devoted to the *Historikerstreit** by Eberhard Jäckel amongst others. One could mention the unparalleled degree of contempt which the Nazi regime had for mankind. Stalin did not, for example, collect the gold fillings from the teeth of the Kulaks and deposit them in the national bank of the Soviet Union. We need not go into all that here, the uniqueness of the Nazi crimes seems clear to me. It is, I think, extremely unfortunate to get embroiled in a dispute about these matters. In the fifties and sixties we had one public argument after the other because some people felt it necessary to claim that the Germans had perhaps only killed two or three million Jews or maybe even only one million. We are in danger of stooping to this undignified level in the present controversy if we begin to argue about these things. I think it is perfectly adequate to state that these crimes are unique, even if certain parallels can be drawn here and there.

Of course there are parallels, but nonetheless we are left with the fact that as Germans we must state that these German crimes were perpetrated by us and not by anybody else. We cannot escape by comparing our crimes with others. Here lies the root of the problem; it raises a number of questions: are we not the same as others; is our youth different although it is growing up like contemporaries in other countries; are we politically cripples; is our thinking maimed; are our public affairs and in some cases also our private lives burdened because these crimes are a crucial part of our history? Another question which should be discussed is the problem of national identity. Do we feel differently from other countries?

This leads us to the problem raised by plans to set up German historical museums†. Habermas mentioned it in his piece. This part of German history should of course not be glossed over in any way. And yet I suspect that the plan to set up a historical

---

* The 'Piper volume' referred to by Christian Meier and other speakers is a book of collected essays and articles dealing with the dispute. These were selected from among the numerous contributions which had appeared in various newspapers and published by Piper Verlag, München, 1987, in a paperback edition entitled *'Historikerstreit' Die Dokumentation der Kontroverse um die Einzigartigkeit der nationalsozialistischen Judenvernichtung.*

† See Stürmer p.80 for the background to this issue.

museum was coupled with the idea that it would provide a normalized access to the recent German past. I entirely disagree with this idea. I cannot imagine that one can look at the positive aspects of German history, which have indeed been numerous, without thinking of the events of the period from 1933 to 1945. Germany brought forth Kant and others, but they did not prevent us from committing not only the greatest acts of stupidity but also the greatest crimes in those Nazi years.

I don't think we will ever get away from this. Reality demands that we be aware of and acknowledge the force of this memory. Nowhere does one come across as many slips of the tongue, blunders, such an astonishing lack of reason as when people speak about this period. It would be worthwhile for a psychiatrist to examine the suppression. It clearly shows that this past is present, that it has penetrated the German consciousness.

This is above all due to German post-war history. We were completely defeated, our country was soon divided and we were faced with two possibilities of identification. On the one hand we could identify with the defeated, that is to say the Germans of 1933–45. The other option was identification with the victors in the Western part of the country. The Western allies had, after all, brought freedom and democracy and we were only too eager to identify with these values. Furthermore by joining NATO and the European Community we had the opportunity of being seen as part of the Western alliance rather than merely as Germans. This leads to difficult psychological problems, problems of identity, which, having existed for forty years, are not so easily cast aside. I therefore think not only ethical considerations, but also sheer realism should compel us to look these facts in the eye and draw the conclusion that because of our history we cannot readily become a normal nation again.

We are confronted with problems of a kind unknown to others. The Japanese do not have the same problems because their post-war history took a different course and because they did not have concentration camps. Whatever they did, they did not exterminate Jews. The Soviets don't have these problems because they are a great power now as before. Glasnost may have tempered the severity of the regime, but we don't know where it is going to lead to. The German situation is therefore unique as regards its post-war development and its present predicament.

HAGEN SCHULZE: A few comments on comparison, *Mittellage*, national identity, and the question of whether history and identity are related or not. I must confess that I believe very strongly in comparing the atrocities of the Nazi regime. It is important to do so and I would advise against disqualifying any such attempt on moral grounds. It is important because only by comparison with other cases which appear to be, or are similar, is it possible to conclude that in some respects the Nazi crimes were unique. Comparison makes it possible to determine what is specific to a particular case and what is general. By recording what is universal we are able to formulate theoretical insights which allow us to fend off or prevent recurrences in the future. Uniqueness is a thing of the past and offers no lessons for the future.

Secondly, the *Mittellage* model. This point has occasionally been over-emphasized in the discussion. I think it is only useful as a theoretical construction which helps to explain typical developments of countries surrounded by many other nations over a long period of time. Polish history shows how useful this procedure is, as it cannot be understood without this factor. English history has, to cite an extreme example of another kind, obviously been greatly influenced by Britain being an island. The same applies to Japan.

Finally, the much more important point concerning national identity and its connection with history. Charles Maier said that history is really only one of several factors in determining identities and that we exaggerate if we use it as the main instrument in determining identity, whilst Christian Meier stated that the Nazi crimes are our crimes. This is a classic case of determining identity through history. I think it is important since as a nation we are only responsible for what happened in the Third Reich because this past has been conveyed through history; this identity is only conveyed through the historical context. That is why the role of history as a creator of identity is not only necessary in itself, but also of great importance politically. That is why I have stressed this point so strongly.

HANS MOMMSEN: I would like to ask, what is normalcy? I have read Professor Gellner's analysis of the nation state in the world and I don't think this is a model which can reliably be used to describe the German situation after the Second World War. I also want to add to what Christian Meier said. Whilst I don't want to go into the subjective position of the historians mentioned, I think it is true to say that their objective function is apologetic. Their stance has been adopted by right wing groups, that means neo-fascist groups. There has been a fundamental shift in the general debate because the post-fascist or neo-fascist groups in the Federal Republic are no longer tabooed. I am disappointed that well-known authors like Hillgruber don't distinguish their views clearly from those expressed in the *Deutsche Nationalzeitung*. This debate is not historiographical. It is a debate about whether the practice upheld by the German political system supported by the Western allies of putting right wing positions under a taboo should be continued or not. Some of the arguments are rather esoteric because we have a clear cut political debate on our hands. This political context cannot be ignored. If it were not, these matters would be far easier. I think some historians fail to see the political context in which they are writing. If they did, they would be more cautious. I certainly believe this to be true of Hillgruber.

JULIUS SCHOEPS: Allow me to make a few remarks as a historian but also as a Jew living in the Federal Republic. I have remained silent in this debate because I did not really know what stance to take. From the beginning I felt that comparability was not what was really at stake in this debate. In my opinion the real issue was the relativization of Nazi crimes. As a result, crucial issues were hardly discussed in this debate. I am thinking for example of the passages in Nolte's articles where he suddenly talks about the Jews declaring war on Hitler, suggesting that Hitler had a right to intern them after all. I am thinking of the monstrous distortion of Kurt Tucholsky's anti-war statements, misquoted in such a way as to express that Tucholsky wished the German bourgeoisie to be killed in gas chambers. Those who are familiar with the subject will know the sources of Nolte's assertions: the extreme right wing publications in the Federal Republic, such as Wilhelm Stäglich's forbidden book *The Auschwitz Myth*, which contains such material, including the misrepresentation of Tucholsky's views. The real problem is that extreme right wing ideas have become acceptable. I think there has been a drastic 'change of climate' in West Germany. It is reflected in this debate, which is not about the problem of comparability, but rather about the much deeper issue of a German historical identity.

GORDON CRAIG: On the point raised at the very beginning about comparison and the legitimacy of certain comparisons. In talking about Nolte we have to remember that he was drawing two kinds of comparison. One is in his polemical articles – the ones which we find most objectionable – where everything boils down to a rather crude comparison between what the Nazis did and what the Soviets did. Then there is the other one with the scholarly note and a more extreme kind of relativization – and this may be even more objectionable. If you look at the pattern of the Nolte trilogy as a whole, he is advancing a different kind of argument; namely that the most traumatic experience in Western civilization has been the impact of industrialization, so traumatic, that it produced violent reactions in many different places. The Nazi reaction is only one of these and it can only be understood if seen in the broader context. This, as developed, is a form of rationalization, if not condonation, of Nazi crimes that I find just as objectionable as the crude comparison between the Soviet and the Nazi experience. While we ask ourselves what constitutes a legitimate comparison we ought to bear in mind not only the newspaper writer Nolte, but the historian Nolte and not forget the trilogy.

JÜRGEN KOCKA: I would like to add a few thoughts on three points made by Charles Maier. Firstly, comparison. The real stumbling block in the debate with Nolte was not his suggestion to compare but his theory, put forward in the form of a question, that the National Socialist race murder was a reaction to the preceding Bolshevik class murders. Nolte did not merely compare, he alleged that there was a causal connection. These are two different intellectual procedures. Interpreting the Holocaust as an understandable or even a meaningful reaction to an alleged threat from the East comes close to a problematic kind of *Sinnstiftung* because, although I do not think Nolte intended it to be so, something which can only be described as senseless is retrospectively given a meaning. This is mere speculation, there is no evidence to support it. In terms of the craft it is wrong. On the other hand it is legitimate that Nolte and others should argue in favour of comparison. But this has never really been disputed, comparisons have always been drawn when dealing with National Socialism in terms of totalitarianism, fascism and other categories. Comparison brings to light differences as well as similarities. The question is, however, who does one wish to compare oneself with? In the

debate about the German *Sonderweg*, ('special path') we traditionally compared ourselves with the West or individual western
countries and in doing so noted certain differences, which were
thought to have facilitated the disintegration of democracy in
Germany in the crisis-ridden years between the wars. The strange
thing about the current debate is that the frame of reference has
changed and that the Stalinist Soviet Union is used for comparison. I do not think there is any definite scientific proof as to
whether one should settle for one country of reference and disregard another and vice versa when comparing. However the
choice is decisive for the outcome of the comparison.

Secondly, a comment on identity. I do not understand, Herr
Stürmer, why the Federal Republic should suddenly be alarmed
that it does not have enough identity. Can one really say that we
do not have enough identity, provided we have a sensible concept
of identity which is both self-critical and pluralistic? I don't think
so. I would join Hans Mommsen in asking, what is the 'normal'
status? Conflict, debates, uncertainties are normal. The lack of
national identity is nothing unusual in large parts of Europe. We
must not talk ourselves into crisis-awareness. I won't deny that
we are faced with special problems in the Federal Republic because
of our recent history, but I don't share this sense of alarm, which
is expressed in the neo-conservative criticism of our alleged lack
of identity. It is for Michael Stürmer and those who share his view
to show us where we lack identity. Furthermore, even if we
did not have enough identity, I doubt very much whether a
dispassionate and critical study of our history could serve to create
identity. For if one looks at history dispassionately, honestly and
as a scholar one very soon meets with conflict. To look into history
may be divisive. The assumption that the study of history can
promote identity has yet to be proved, particularly in our case.

Finally, what form should our rhetoric take if we as historians
comment on these subjects which are by no means only historical?
Above all, we should argue with the means at our disposal, that
is to say, by using historical evidence and by a process of historical
examination.

This enables us to distinguish between subjective speculation
and legitimate interpretation, between political resentment and
historical truth. The principles of our craft can help rationalize
public debates, even if these debates are political in nature, as is
the case with the *Historikerstreit*. But to achieve that we have to
define clearly what we mean. We must not only ask questions,

we must try to answer them. We must avoid ambiguous rhetoric even if it sells well in the media. As scholars we cannot afford to indulge in the kind of journalistic brilliance for which one has to pay with superficiality and inaccuracy. If historians had adhered to these principles, certain misunderstandings and polarizations in the recent debate could have been avoided.

I don't share Julius Schoeps' concern. I think the results of the *Historikerstreit* so far show that the critical powers of historical scholarship are by no means all that underdeveloped. From my point of view the results are not bad.

MICHAEL STÜRMER: I think the terms 'identity', let alone *Sinnstiftung*, endowment with meaning, are confusing and confused. They do in fact differ greatly in meaning. To identify with a cause is something personal and historians should be reluctant to do so. But identity is a different thing. My concept of identity, and I think it is largely shared by Helmut Schmidt, Fernand Braudel and others, had nothing to do with saying: we have enough, or we have too little identity. Identity is not a commodity people have, it is a constant wrestling with the past, the present and the future. It is part of the human condition after the fall of God and the decline of Religion. It is, very generally, an attempt to define one's personal or collective place in time and space. You cannot do this without knowing where you are and where you came from. This permanent search for where we are going is part of the Western heritage, it is part of the human predicament.

After the war the Germans – fortunately or unfortunately – found and defined their new identity through the model of anti-totalitarianism because it made them shareholders in the Western victory over the Nazis. They were on the right side, on the side of the stronger battalions. For the past ten years, however, we have slowly been drifting towards a different paradigm. Its communist provenance dates back to the 1930s and 1940s. It opens up a perspective different from that of the *Grundgesetz*, the Basic Constitutional Law. I cannot see what good it can lead to.

Am I being alarmist? I am aware of this search because one cannot escape it. If you think you can escape, you are simply closing the doors to the outside world. Let me remind you of two impressive remarks made by Helmut Schmidt. In his final address to the Bundestag, Schmidt said: '*Wir sind ein gefährdetes Volk*', 'we are an endangered people, and God help us if we don't know our history well enough, if we ignore large parts of it.' I would like to add a footnote to this. In the sixties and seventies we abolished the teaching of history in many of our schools, especially in Hesse, and that included lessons on what really went on in the Third Reich. Instead, children were taught about fascism and theories of fascism which regard fascism as the inevitable result of liberalism, pluralism and capitalism. The second quote of which I am particularly fond is from a speech Schmidt made on 8 May 1985: 'In the long run no nation can live without a historical identity. If our German history were merely regarded as one single chain of crimes and failure, our nation could be shaken and its future could be at stake.' Schmidt is the last person to be alarmist; he ought to be taken seriously.

RALF DAHRENDORF: I notice that with the exception of Charles Maier and Gordon Craig all those who have spoken so far are Germans more or less involved in the debate. I am therefore going to call on a number of other speakers now to see whether we can find a somewhat different, or wider perspective. I would be intrigued to know whether Saul Friedlander feels that the debate has been of some use. After all, he triggered it off.

SAUL FRIEDLANDER: I would not consider myself as having set the debate in motion. That would be too much honour. I think a certain climate pervaded and it is in this context that my little spark created some controversy. Without this environment the spark would have gone unnoticed. The interesting thing here is the question of why now? What are the dynamics of this evolution, was it useful in any way? I wonder if it didn't clarify some things which would have been left unsaid for some time. Maybe it is better to have things out in the open, to be able to discuss them, to disagree – and one does disagree very strongly here. We are not dealing with a theoretical matter. Theoretical questions are our daily bread. We would not be here if it were only a theoretical discussion. I think everyone here feels deeply concerned.

If this debate has been useful in any way, it is as a catalyst. After forty years it has, for whatever reason, brought to the surface something which had been in the air for two or three years and which must now be confronted. That is why the general public is following it with such intensity. This would not be the case if we were dealing with a purely theoretical argument. Everybody feels that there is something very basic in it. We should try and pinpoint this basic aspect and not opt for the easy way out by getting involved in theory and asking about comparison and rhetoric.

LORD ANNAN: If I speak it will be like somebody walking in hobnail boots across this discussion because I feel very prosaic about the problem which I have been listening to with absolute fascination. On the question of comparison there seems to me to be no great problem. Leaving aside primitive times, in which tribes exterminated the tribe into whose territory they were moving, (or, if they did not exterminate them, they reduced such males as were left alive to slavery) if we look at modern times, i.e. from before the French Revolution, the Holocaust is surely a unique event. Here was a regime determined to exterminate a race not merely within the boundaries of the state itself, but within any territories into which that state moved. I don't see how the uniqueness of the Nazi aim can be denied. While Nolte may never have exactly denied its uniqueness, he was attempting, in comparing to it Stalin's extermination of the Kulaks, to mitigate it, or in some way to make it appear as yet another event of man's perennial inhumanity to man. I can't accept that.

But I then move on to say that all nations live with guilt of one kind or another. My own generation in Britain lived with a mild form of guilt. This took the form of shame about what happened in the nineteenth century industrial revolution, the poverty, the slums, and unemployment. This mild form of guilt affected our writing of history, and certainly our way of looking at politics. From 1945 until 1979 there was a consensus in British politics that we should try to eliminate this stain on our national life. We showed our sense of guilt by the form economics and the form industrial relations took. I was interested that Nolte himself refers to economics and industrialization as producing situations which create guilt in countries. There was incidentally another form of guilt which the British lived with – guilt about imperialism and the way they had treated their colonies and India. The fact that some nations live with a sense of guilt – though I always think that the French are remarkably able to live without that sense – doesn't alter the fact that there is a special problem in Germany.

The British themselves sometimes show signs of involving themselves in Germany's guilt. The journalist Tom Bower has made his speciality the examination of the British and American involvement in allowing war criminals and the vilest form of Nazi to escape from Germany to South America and elsewhere. The

Anglo-Americans connived at such escapes because these criminals had been able to help in identifying communist cells in
Western Europe. Although Bower grossly over-estimates the
ability of the allies immediately after the war to round up all the
war criminals of this kind, one must admit that he is right to point
out that the Western allies were not without some willingness to
fudge issues on the particular responsibility for bringing home to
the world at large the fact that an attempt had been made
to murder a whole race.

We should be careful when we say this is a historical problem.
We should also regard it as a political problem. It would be
monstrous if the whole matter were swept under the carpet. And
yet it worries me that when something that should be treated as
a problem for scholarly research gets treated as a political issue.
I do not like the politicization of history. I associate that with the
way the Communist Party treats history.

The question of how guilty the present generation is opens up
an entirely new field. It's there that I become very much more
sceptical. I always carry in my mind the words of Burke that 'I
do not know the method of drawing up an indictment against a
whole people.' Burke knew how concrete life is and how complicated and complex a question it is to identify who knew, who
guessed, who never could possibly have known that the Jews
were being exterminated. It is perfectly clear to me that you
cannot say that every single German living at that particular
moment in time was involved in this appalling tragedy.

ISAIAH BERLIN: I would like to ask a slightly loaded question.
Obviously it's sensible to say, if uniqueness of a phenomenon,
particularly of a horrifying phenomenon, is examined we mustn't
rush to the conclusion that it's unique in human history before
we have compared it to other phenomena which in some ways
may resemble it. That is what is being applied to the Holocaust.
But think of unique events like the French Revolution. Nobody
went about saying, is the French Revolution really unique, does
it really resemble the 'Glorious Revolution', Cromwell and the
Puritans, something which happened in Athens in 405, the
Roman Principate, and if so, what political conclusions should be
drawn? Even with the Russian Revolution, which some of its
makers thought analogous to the French Revolution, you don't
come across writings either for or against, trying to emphasize its
uniqueness or non-uniqueness, its similarity or dissimilarity to

what went on before. Therefore there must be a good deal more to the question of uniqueness – the 'placing in context' of this event than a mere historical assessment of an objective kind. It has a conspicuously political motive. That is my impression. I feel sure it is one that is shared by others.

FELIX GILBERT: I would like to raise some questions about historical method. Nobody will deny that the Holocaust is the most terrible crime committed not only in the twentieth century, but probably in modern times and perhaps before. We must consider that the breakdown of the legal system in Germany happened earlier, in the spring of 1933 and went on progressively from there. I suppose I'm the only one here who was an adult in 1933 when the Nazis came to power. The point I want to make is that the doors were gradually opened to this unbelievably cruel and inhuman illegality which took place in the later years of the Nazi regime. In examining the beginning and the gradual extension of the advance into illegality a discussion can be more instructive than focusing exclusively on the Holocaust. As to national identity, it certainly is an important issue but national identity is something which changes steadily. In order to discuss it in a productive way its historical development and background must be fully investigated. The influence of the general political situation, the changes it brings about, the adjustment it requires are all important elements which must be taken into account when dealing with national identity. I don't under any circumstances want to deny that the issues with which we are concerned are political issues. But at the same time I do think that they can be answered, discussed on a political basis only when the historical questions are fully investigated.

HAROLD JAMES: I wonder whether we aren't dealing with two questions at the same time. The first of those questions is about how a nation comes to terms with enormous crimes and enormous evil, how you integrate crimes into your picture of the nation, and how the past affects your view of your own identity in the present. But there's another question that I find very puzzling and which I think contributes to the confusion and the animosity raised by this issue in Germany and outside Germany. That question is: what is a nation with regard to the German question? The Germans have defined nation and national identity in the past, in the nineteenth century, in two ways that touch on the debate here. First of all in a comparative way, in that from the eighteenth century onwards Germans looked to other nations as models of how they might behave, how they might develop. They looked to France, they looked to England, they looked to Italy, to ancient Greece even – the famous 'Tyranny of Greece over Germany'. So there is a continual comparative aspect. But unlike Britain or France, Germans have a difficulty in that they can't find an identity in particular institutions. They have to look outside, to import their sense of meaning and their sense of identity. In Britain you can talk about formation of national identity around the development of parliamentary institutions and in France after the Revolution there is the consensus, at least among the centre and the left, that the revolutionary legacy is important. In Germany there are no institutions of that kind so you look to something mistier, vaguer.

The other way that the Germans look is to history. The historical element has always been more important in making myths about national identity than in any other country, certainly in Western Europe. This is the story of the *Historikerstreit* of the 1850s and 1860s when people talked about the Holy Roman Empire and whether it was good or whether it had a detrimental effect on national development.

These two areas, the comparative area and the historical area, have always been at the centre of forming national identity and in Germany they have always been appallingly vague. That is why, if in addition you integrate into that a sense of guilt about the past, you are faced with a great difficulty, which seems to me to be irresolvable. The problem arises simply when anyone starts talking about what it is to be German, it is probably a concept that should be avoided.

JOACHIM FEST: Charles Maier has called the *Historikerstreit* a very important debate, but I am under the impression that he nonetheless disputes its preconditions. Maier thinks it was wrong and damaging to publish Nolte's article, but, after all, it was this piece that triggered everything off. At the time we asked ourselves whether we should publish it; the decision was by no means easy. I disagree with Nolte on several points even though Jürgen Kocka claims the contrary in the Piper book, where he states, for example, that I supported the Chaim Weizmann theory. That was new to me.

In the end, we decided to publish the piece because I think that an issue like this which is of considerable interest and significance should be aired in public. Contrary to what some people apparently believe, it should not be the privilege of specialists to expound such questions. Of course we were aware that the article would meet with response, considerable response even. No one expected a *Historikerstreit* though. I still wonder why this dispute came about and why it took place at this particular time. We should perhaps explore this further, as it seems to me to be one of the more important aspects of the dispute.

By way of contrast, or perhaps even because of this, I find the excitement about much of what dominates the debate somewhat artificial and hypothetical. I am thinking for example of everything that has been said about the apparent attempts to relativize or minimize the moral reprehension of the Third Reich. It cannot seriously be disputed that the moral questions regarding the Third Reich have long been settled, and I cannot think of anyone at all who has tried to bring them up again. Charles Maier now states that the singularity of these crimes has been 'trivialized'. I don't agree and I can't see where this has occurred. Neither can I share the worry that this debate might have this effect. Like all German participants here I have taken part in numerous discussions in the Federal Republic since this argument began. In the course of these I gained quite the opposite impression: the moral sensibility towards the events of those years has increased, possibly even as a result of this dispute. Where is there proof of trivialization or of these presumed effects? Or does mere comparison with other crimes trivialize the Nazi crimes, that is to say minimize them, make them morally more acceptable?

Wolfgang Mommsen has raised another point. He said that the German public has not faced up to the past during the last forty years. I think German historians have been living a lie, *Lebenslüge*.

Allow me to speak about myself for a moment. I was not originally very interested in contemporary history. But my whole career, as I had planned it in my teens, was changed, even distorted by the Nazi years. Since 1953 when I began my career as a journalist I have not really dealt with anything other than this period. And I am not the only one to have been affected in this way. A whole generation of journalists has devoted innumerable books, articles, radio and television programmes to the problems posed by the Third Reich. One cannot claim that the public did not face up to this. On the contrary, it followed these discussions with interest and sympathy and even with passion.

The public has also been silent though. Sometimes this behaviour may even seem indolent, but in my opinion it is not. The attitude is rather one of helplessness in the face of publications by historians who have never understood, or never wanted to understand that this public exists and that they also have responsibilities towards it. All their texts are written in a haughty and hermetic manner, they are inaccessible and are directed at a small group of colleagues. I don't want to criticize this on principle, the method is surely legitimate. But I don't think it is legitimate to reproach the public for being indifferent when one is shutting oneself off from that public. Historians writing about the Nazi period have denied it a language. Instead they invented complicated theories so that nobody can recognize reality in their works; nor will anyone find the morality which these historians lay claim to, it only crops up as a hollow term. I think all this stands in the way of understanding rather than promoting it. In these texts history comes across as something very remote which is not worth remembering. If this is so, then historians should not complain that the public has failed.

Finally, a more fundamental thought which brings us back to the starting point. Shortly after Nolte's piece appeared, I spoke to a Jewish friend who lives in the Federal Republic and is very successful there. He told me that he firmly opposed Nolte's theories, he thought they were quite wrong. Nonetheless, this friend did not want to challenge the right to raise these questions. He only felt that a German should not have the right to expound them. I was astonished by this statement and asked him if that meant that truth had a nationality. He answered: 'Yes. Of course it has. At any rate, Germans are not entitled to certain subjects.' At the time I took this to be a somewhat exaggerated punch line. But a few weeks later the same opinion was expressed in a comment on the historians' debate in the *Neue Zürcher Zeitung*. I think this touches on fundamental questions. The various answers to them could also reveal to what extent this dispute is political and whether academic research merely serves as an alibi or as a substitute in this context.

HANS MOMMSEN: I believe that the *Historikerstreit*, or whatever lies behind it, has meant that aspects of the Nazi past can now be dealt with on a broader scale. This has a disadvantage. It means having to grapple with the neo- or post-fascists yet again. This will preoccupy us. I am sure it was Nolte's intention to force this opening up. We have already touched on the question of whether he really had to go about it the way he did.

RALF DAHRENDORF: Herr Stürmer would like to know what you mean by neo- or post-fascist.

HANS MOMMSEN: I mean quite simply the *Deutsche National-zeitung*, I mean Otto Ernst Remer, the editor of a periodical called *Der Bismarck-Deutsche*, I mean all the literature which is classified by the Office for the Protection of the Constitution. I leave it to you to decide to what extent certain neo-conservative groupings should be included.

I think the debate has changed the paradigm, in that historians of National Socialism have been concentrating on Auschwitz of late. Before they only did so to a limited extent. That is also linked with the fact that the general interest is shifting from the early period of Nazi rule to the years of the Second World War. This is ambivalent, however, as Nolte's case in particular shows that there is a growing tendency to absolutize the crimes against the Jews, to take them out of the political context and to present them as the work of a relatively small group within the Nazi system or, as Nolte is inclined to do, to think of it as something which went on in Hitler's head alone, thus freeing others from blame. I don't think historians intended this, but it is essential to bear in mind the political environment which produces these trends. I need only mention David Irving and the response he meets with in Germany. In this respect I think Nolte's bringing things to a head is misleading and alarming because it is capable of setting back the general discussion and the level of scholarship considerably.

CHARLES MAIER: I would like to link Isaiah Berlin's question with Joachim Fest's remarks. As many people have pointed out, one interesting aspect of this debate is that no one denies that this genocide was an awful crime. The so-called revisionists have merely said that other regimes carried out similar policies. But some say, why should we worry if certain historians stress comparability? Does it make the Nazi genocide any less appalling if one stresses its comparability with, say, the Soviet purges? In fact, comparability is psychologically at the heart of the debate. It was clearly the neuralgic point at which this debate began and burst into public. I don't stress the issue of comparison just out of a theoretical need or desire. We have to be very careful about what comparison is and what it involves if we are going to do our duty, especially in terms of leading public opinion to pose certain questions.

Sir Isaiah Berlin asked what was so special about the Holocaust. I agree with the thrust of his query. Americans can discuss slavery without a sense of oppression. To some extent we had the good fortune that a series of political events in the sixties continued a process of trying to repair or overcome a burdened past. I think Ernst Nolte feels that if the Holocaust is thought to be really singular the chapter can't ever be closed. It is like the wound in *Parsifal*. It just won't heal – although it does in the end, of course. There is a feeling expressed by some Germans and shared by certain Americans: can't we forget all this, why are we being hassled by history, to use American slang? The mood is: the era of prohibition and restriction on public discourse should be over and done with. But the point is that one can insist the Final Solution was in fact unique without feeling that Germany can never be a normal country. I travel there frequently; I feel West Germany is a normal country. It has debated civic problems, it is concerned about its European orientation, its Western orientation. I feel very strongly about the specialness of Nazi crimes, but as an observer it doesn't make me think there is an unhealable wound. Theodor Adorno once wrote that one had to work through the past, *aufarbeiten*, to overcome it. I don't think that the Nolte position allows the working through of the past.

As regards the publication of Nolte's article by the *Frankfurter Allgemeine*, I recognize that it must have been a difficult decision. My comment would be that an editor must be aware that an article can introduce trajectories of argumentation that are not always intended (although in fact I think in Nolte's case they were intended). Let me quote a translation of part of Nolte's article, not the one that's usually offered: 'The situation of the Federal Republic, characterized by the past which does not pass away, can lead to a qualitatively new and unprecedented situation where the national socialist past becomes a negative myth of absolute evil, prevents relevant revisions, and is therefore hostile to scholarship. Simultaneously this has the political consequence that those who fought most decisively against this absolute evil were the most correct.' Ernst Nolte is, I believe, arguing that the Resistance cannot be questioned as long as we have that view of the past. Such an implication certainly emerges from Hillgruber's book. Now, if you really wish to say that the conspirators of 20

July 1944 were wrong – all right. But the consequences of calling into question the Resistance to Nazism should be explicitly confronted. It should be understood that words and arguments have trajectories.

Finally, let me respond to Hagen Schulze's indirect response to me. You cannot neatly separate what is singular in a comparison from what is common. Comparison always involves genus and species. Aristotle gave us the logic; comparison requires two mental operations at once. Is it true that historians sacrifice their capacity to make moral judgements if they deal with 'unique' events? From the viewpoint of moral judgement, we are told, we need be concerned only with what is comparable; we can't be morally concerned about the singular because the singular can never happen again. Every genocide is singular, every war is singular, crimes are singular. But complex behaviour has singular and comparable elements. To say the Holocaust was singular is not to say it cannot be classified as wicked. We cannot just say, for example, that it was mad, or that since we cannot fathom psychopaths, we needn't worry about them. Psychopaths walk about in the street, they shoot people. We say they were crazy, we can't diagnose them in advance. But psychopathology repeats itself, and it's too simple to say that we need only be concerned with the comparable.

FRITZ STERN: Let me make a few unconnected comments as they occurred to me whilst listening to the discussion. A footnote to what Joachim Fest said. I can understand the difficulties, the real anguish he and his colleagues must have felt when the question of whether or not to publish Nolte's article came up. I can certainly see the argument of free speech on the one hand. I can also see the argument from the famous American judicial decision that one does not have the right to shout fire in a crowded theatre, that this is not an example of free speech. I wonder whether the atmosphere in Germany had changed to such an extent that the article with the phrase 'was it an Asiatic deed' could have been published without it being inflammatory, but it was probably right to publish it. It seems to me that some historians who were active in the so-called *Historikerstreit* – I'll explain why I say so-called *Historikerstreit* later – I won't say in support of Nolte, but on his side, in a certain sense achieved the opposite of what they intended. The intention in general was to make it, as it were, easier for the Germans to live with their past, an intention that I can understand. The result was that suddenly all sorts of memories were stirred up, unease was felt particularly in the outside world, but obviously, as the discussion here shows, not only in the outside world. I don't think it is a historian's debate. Usually historical debates are about interpretation, we also argue about sources, about different methods of investigation and so on. This debate has moved at a dangerously abstract level on the one hand, and consists of polemical nit-picking on the other. It became perilously *ad hominem*. I will not go into whether there is a question of national style involved here or not. I do want very much to support what Hans Mommsen said, that there is a further danger in isolating the Holocaust and saying that is the single most important crime. Felix Gilbert was right to remind us of 1933.

I would like to pick up one comment that Lord Annan made. He said that the French are remarkably free of guilt. At first I found this appropriate and amusing. Then I remembered the Algerian war and the response within France to it, the sense of responsibility that many Frenchmen felt for the torture that was going on. Compare that to behaviour in Germany in 1933. We're not talking about 1945, we shouldn't be. The destruction which took place in 1933 was still in the context of a regime that was unsure of itself. The Nazis were nervous about any sign of opposition. So a discussion about guilt should not be focused on the Holocaust alone but on the failure to protest in 1933. It occurs to me that the more we talk about guilt, the more I'm convinced that this whole debate is really psychological and political and not so much historical. I haven't thought this through at all, but I'm suggesting it: guilt and self-pity are not unrelated and we could be dealing with a phenomenon here where guilt is associated with a heavy and dangerous dose of self-pity. That would be of no use to anybody.

My last observation is in the form of a question. Since 1950 or so, certainly since the Fischer debate, the German historical profession has, it seems to me, come up with a remarkable degree of pluralistic thinking within a given consensus. I wonder whether what is wrongly labelled the *Historikerstreit* is a sign that that consensus, as well as a broader consensus in the Federal Republic, is in danger of disintegration.

SAMUEL ETTINGER: I would like to follow the line taken by Fritz Stern and say that it is not a *Historikerstreit* despite the fact that the majority of the participants are historians. When in the early 1880s Theodor Mommsen criticized Treitschke for being anti-semitic no one spoke about a *Historikerstreit*. It was a political and moral issue. The same applies here. The debate is important educationally, politically, morally but it's certainly not a polemic of historians. Not only because methodological questions were not raised but because it was faulty from the historical point of view. I agree that you can compare everything with everything. You can compare Hitler with Atilla's Huns, after all, Stalin was called Genghis Khan with a telephone. In my opinion it does not make much sense to compare Genghis Khan with Stalin, but still, you can do it. The condition for doing so, however, is that you study Stalin and Genghis Khan before you start comparing them.

The fault of this discussion lies in the fact that none of the participants actually knows enough about the problems of the Soviet Union and they compare Hitler and Stalin only on the basis of some kind of moralistic generalization. Here is an example I took from the Piper volume: The *Vertreibung*, expulsion, or *Vernichtung*, extermination, of the Kulaks, the Russian peasants. Habermas used the word *Vertreibung*, expulsion. Everyone was indignant, even Christian Meier, who was very objective in his presentation, was appalled that Habermas used the term expulsion for the persecution of the Kulaks. But who among the participants of the *Historikerstreit* has studied the problem of collectivisation in depth? Hillgruber says there is a difference between studying Germany and studying Russia because we don't have the facts on Russia. And yet he compares. The people who are knowledgeable in the field know that it was an expulsion and not an extermination because Stalin was not interested in exterminating the peasants. He was interested in slave labour and in settlement. To say on the one hand that we don't have enough historical material and on the other hand to make comparisons is very dubious from a scholarly point of view.

Secondly, there is the question of quotations. Quotations from Lacis, who was the First Cheka Chief; Tucholsky, the satirist and journalist, and Theodor Kaufmann (who knows who Theodor Kaufmann was?) were used as historical sources. Can an assorted collection of this kind serve as a basis for serious scholarly analysis, the starting point for a claim that poor Hitler was so frightened by the 'Asiatic deeds' of the Bolsheviks that he started to exterminate Jewish children? All this without taking into account the historical development of the relationship between Germany and the Soviet Union, the military co-operation during the twenties which was well known to the German general staff and to Hitler, Tukhachevsky's speech which was applauded at a meeting of the general staff of Germany in 1935 for its anti-Western remarks. Then there are the negotiations between Stalin and Hitler from '36 or '37 onwards which brought a rapprochement and led to the dismissal of Jewish diplomats and other public officials up until the division of Poland in 1939. I take exception to what Professors Mommsen and Stern said about the Holocaust as a singular crime. It's certainly not the only crime of the Nazis, they were criminal in various fields. They destroyed the legal state in Germany, they persecuted minorities. Nevertheless, there is a difference between all the other crimes and the persecution of the Jews. You could have been a former Communist member of the Reichstag and survive under the Nazi regime until 1945, but you could not have been a two-year-old Jewish girl and survive. I think that's the difference.

FRITZ STERN: I obviously agree with what Ettinger has just said. What I had in mind was that the question of responsibility and guilt can be observed more clearly in 1933 when Germany was still a society that was three quarters closed and one quarter open, if you want to put it that way, and that the sense of responsibility and therefore the sense of guilt must also be investigated at that point. Opposition or protest in the early months would not have demanded martyrdom and could have been quite effective.

RALF DAHRENDORF: I agree. Felix Gilbert also raised the difficult issue that taking the Holocaust totally out of context could be seen as a form of apology. He reminded us of the context in which this happened.

SAMUEL ETTINGER: There is another lacuna in the historians' debate. That is the failure to discuss the influence and the history of anti-semitism in dealing with the problems of Germany. Anti-semitism was an extremely serious phenomenon in European history in general and in German history in particular. The sources of European and German anti-semitism as one of the major factors of the Nazi policies towards the Jews should be dealt with. This wasn't done in the *Historikerstreit*.

JULIUS SCHOEPS: I would like to stress a seminal factor in the *Historikerstreit*: The historians who caused this dispute are men in their sixties, that is, men who were old enough to be in the Hitler youth, Hitlerjugend; men who were perhaps soldiers in the war; men for whom the collapse of the Third Reich turned into a trauma which is inextricably linked to the key terms Holocaust and Auschwitz. Nolte's reaction is, I think, typical of this generation of scholars. Contrary to some historians who assert that Germans should not ask such questions at all, I believe that Germans must ask them. But there is no need for slanted questions and ambiguous statements which whitewash German history. Unfortunately, questions of this kind were posed in the *Historikerstreit*; such assertions were made. If historians are suggesting today that Hitler had a right to intern the Jews, they may be tempted to suggest tomorrow that he had a right to kill the Jews. This is why it is crucial to discuss such moral, political, ethnic lies.

Why is this debate taking place now and not before? I think that the debate is the result of a specific development in post-war Germany. If you look at what historians have written since 1945 about the Holocaust, you will see that in the first decades there are almost no publications by German historians. The important studies were written in the United States, in England, in Israel, in France, everywhere except Germany. We must bear this in mind.

Another seminal fact should be noted: After 1945 not a single university chair for German-Jewish history was established in the Federal Republic. There was no chair for Holocaust studies in West Germany! But there are many such professorships in the United States. No major changes occurred until the end of the seventies. A recent survey, which examined the course schedules of all West German universities, revealed that there are academic institutions which even today do not include courses in Holocaust studies in their curricula. Bonn University is a particularly striking example. Even by 1980 this university did not offer courses in Holocaust studies. The subject was only introduced recently, it is however, being taught within a very historical context.

MICHAEL STÜRMER: Are you saying that no lectures on National Socialism have been held in German universities?

JULIUS SCHOEPS: No. I'm saying that there were no courses on anti-semitism and on the Holocaust. This specific aspect of recent history has been deliberately ignored.

MICHAEL STÜRMER: There were and there are innumerable courses and lectures on the 'Third Reich'. But the topics you name would seem too specialized for a three-hour lecture course lasting one semester, when a student, to pass his finals, has to cover much more ground than just German history from 1933 to 1945. It does not suit the style of German universities.

JULIUS SCHOEPS: An opinion such as the one expressed by Professor Stürmer now is precisely the problem. I think the Holocaust is one of the central issues, and we all agree that it is a traumatic issue. We have to deal with it. In West Germany we have only recently begun to discuss it. Some historians have finally taken the matter up, and this is why the *Historikerstreit* has become acute.

WOLFGANG MOMMSEN: I would like to comment on what Joachim Fest very pointedly called *Die Lebenslüge der Historiker*, the lie historians have been living. I agree, there has been a time-lag. The historical profession started to deal with recent German history rather late. The process only began in 1958 with Karl Dietrich Bracher's book, and if you look at the period beyond Weimar then the serious assessment of Germany's past began with the Fischer debate in 1959. The time-lag also applies to the response of the public. I am not that far away from Fest's observation about attempts by historians and journalists to bring the message across. In some ways, however, we didn't succeed, or we succeeded only to a limited extent in reaching the general public, particularly in reaching the generation directly involved in National Socialist rule.

For the last few years I have been collecting historical information about the historical awareness of people not directly connected with these matters. That includes the proverbial 'man in the street'. Having been silent about history for a long time people are suddenly beginning to talk about the past again. What they say is often hair-raising, for in many cases nationalist or even fascist views are being expressed. In fact there is a gap between what may be called the official or published notion of the past and the opinion of some members of the public on the subject. At the moment we are faced with the new phenomenon that people are all of a sudden interested in history again. The public wants to hear about German history again; German and not European histories are in demand. Suddenly publications on problems of German national identity go into five or six editions. This is not the result of political manipulation, it is a spontaneous phenomenon. However, difficulties arise when the question of how to locate National Socialism in what may be called an ideal continuity of German history is raised. The real issue is how we can, or whether we ought to reconstruct a German history of which Germans need no longer feel ashamed. This seems to be what the public wants. Professional historians have adopted a cautious stance on this issue, perhaps it is not cautious enough.

It is in this context of evaluating events of recent German history that it matters whether one says that the Russians were the first to commit genocide on a grand scale and that we only followed this example, or whether it is true to say that the German bourgeoisie was so afraid of Bolshevism, and rightly so, that they had no other option but to support the National Socialists. That is the new message contained in Nolte's various statements. Behind all this is the attempt to formulate what may be called a new paradigm of German history; this is bound to have considerable political ramifications. Politicians were quick to grasp this point, even quicker than the historians. From Johannes Rau to Franz Josef Strauß politicians suddenly discovered they could perhaps win elections with national historical arguments.

I was directly affected by Nolte's article because, not knowing that he had been asked to speak about 'The past that does not pass away' at the Römerberg Gespräche in Frankfurt, I agreed to give a talk on this very subject; consequently Nolte felt disinvited. I would have been prepared to give up the title at once had I known the consequence. The important thing was that Nolte deliberately cloaked his argument in a language which implied an attack on the Left. This was clearly a political act on his part and it triggered off the dispute. Nolte had every right to do as he did. Under the circumstances everybody knew or could have known that the battle being fought was one about competing Geschichtsbilder, images of Germany's past; it is about the search for a new paradigm to replace the critical liberal one which focuses on the question of why German history led to 1933.

RALF DAHRENDORF: I have followed the debate with great personal interest and involvement. And yet I do not find it easy even now to say precisely what the debate is about, although I share some of the emotions which have been expressed here. I cannot imagine that this intensity can have been generated by Jürgen Habermas' well-known nonchalance in quoting from other authors. I cannot even imagine that this intensity was generated by Ernst Nolte's ability to mix metaphysics and history, or indeed Hillgruber's obsession with certain events he has personally experienced – and don't we all have such obsessions. There must be something else. In my view this something else is indeed political, it has very little to do with history and has much more to do with a process of redefining political positions in the Federal Republic. It can be observed both on the political level, in events like Bitburg, and on the intellectual level. It so happens that it has surfaced in this debate.

To me the most striking feature of Habermas' initial article is the passage at the end about constitutional patriotism. Here is the man who to many stands for an ideology which seeks to change the system, who is seen by many as having helped incite the troubles of 1968 and who thought in terms which were contrary to the acceptance of the Federal Republic as the unit within which one operates, as a civil society worth defending. And now, this man who is always seen as opposing these values, suddenly espouses them.

It has always struck me as one of the curious aspects of the Federal Republic that it has never really had a normal party of the Right. In fact the Centre Right of the political spectrum was constituted by people who accepted the Federal Republic as such, who did not talk about the nation in a wider sense or about reunification, who accepted the integration of the Federal Republic into the European community and into NATO. They have put the Left in that strange position which it has occupied almost ever since the State came into existence. Despite Herbert Wehner's great speech accepting the integration of the Federal Republic into the West, there was a lingering non-acceptance of the Federal Republic within the Social Democratic Party. I am not talking about extremists, I am talking about the main political groupings of the country. Scepticism about the Federal Republic lingered and it told even in the motives of some, not all, of those connected with the early period of *Ostpolitik*.

I have always wondered whether this peculiar political constellation could last. To put it crudely: what has happened is that under Helmut Kohl the German Right has turned away from Adenauer and has begun to look for a different definition of its own basic political stance. Somehow or other the identity question is important to them. Surprisingly, those of whom I would have expected it least are at the same time suddenly beginning to defend the Federal Republic and the constitution. We are faced with a process of redefining German political positions, rather than with a specific or disciplined discussion about the events of the Holocaust and Nazi Germany. This involves a major change not only in the views of historians but in the political discourse of the country.

It can't have escaped anyone's notice that this discussion is more than an exchange of different views among scholars committed to the same scholarly values. There is an additional ingredient. This lends an intensity and gravity to the debate which is sometimes worrying and which must be rather puzzling to some of those who are not part of it. I don't propose to dig too far and try to uncover the deep underlying differences, but I suggest we devote some time to these issues.

HANS MOMMSEN: We have spoken about the far-reaching consequences of the historians' dispute, but we should also look into the reason why it broke out at that particular time and not earlier. I don't think it is possible to find a definite answer. There seems to be a connection between the activities of a relatively broad group of intellectuals which could be called neo-conservative and the current debate on restoring German national consciousness. This group complains about the German neurosis and says that there is a pathological development which makes Germans think less in national terms than neighbouring nations. This is an underlying tendency in German public opinion which goes back to the late sixties and should be seen in conjunction with the debate about the reinterpretation of German history in the twentieth century.

In order to analyze this one has to look at the German intellectual scene in recent years and examine specific political interests and the alleged legitimacy of the political system. The specific difficulty of the German conservatives has already been mentioned. Their political position is unclear and I think the flight into history, the attempt to develop something like a concept of history must be seen in this political context.

MICHAEL STÜRMER: So far, the quality of our discussion has suffered from two main weaknesses. One is the absence of the two philosophers who are constantly being quoted but are unable to explain or defend themselves. It cannot be helped, but it makes things difficult. The other weakness lies in the fact that there are a number of contradictions which cannot only be explained with the usual muddle-headedness of academic debate but must be ascribed to real political differences.

I still fail to understand the word *Vergleich* and the profound implications it seems to have in this context. In German *Vergleich*, comparison, has two meanings. It is an extremely ambiguous word. In colloquial German *Vergleich* means that two things are equal. In an intellectual context it means that two things are similar but unequal and that's why there is a point in comparing the dimensions in which they are similar.

I also fail to understand why Nolte is accused of belittling Hitler's atrocities by comparing them to Stalin's. Nor do I see how anyone who has ever studied the Weimar Republic, its origin and lasting traumas, can overlook the fact that from 1917 onwards most Germans were indeed traumatized, while some had a new vision of the future, in both cases on account of the Bolshevik Revolution. There is extensive literature on how the SPD and the trade unions reacted to the Bolshevik Revolution, not to mention the bourgeoisie, the nobility, the clergy, etc.

To disregard this is to disregard one of the birth traumas of republican Germany. People like Friedrich Ebert were traumatized, but they never dreamt of accusing the Jews of having brought about their trauma. Hitler certainly was traumatized, he was traumatized by many things, for example, by what happened in Munich during the *Räterepublik* and its aftermath. That has never been challenged by any serious scholar. I don't know what the implications of this were for what Hitler and the Nazis did later, but these traumas should be taken as an established historical fact. The Austrians, the Hungarians, the Germans and many others were all traumatized because they lived through troubled times.

Wolfgang Mommsen has asserted the Germanness of Nazism. At the same time he is concerned about a new interest in writing German history. How can you assert the Germanness of Nazism without writing German history? Writing German history doesn't necessarily mean writing nationalist German history. Does he propose to condemn German history without studying it? Surely not. Furthermore, it is important to have a comprehensive view of German history in its European context if one refuses to see that Germany has always been situated at the centre of the European system. That is one of the facts of life of German history, as it is one of the basic facts of American history that America is a continental nation and one of the basic facts about British history that Britain is an island nation.

That does not mean that Germany's fate is determined by its geography alone, but it adds to an understanding of Germany's destiny or tragedy. As Ralf Dahrendorf pointed out, it is indeed an ambiguous situation. In economic terms, being at the centre of everything enriches a nation; in strategic terms, matters are more awkward, dangerous and tempting. You can't deal with European history and leave out Germany. I fail to see how one could write a history of Germany and leave out the European context. It is intellectually weak and politically infamous to denounce an approach that looks beyond the class struggle at the interplay of political and ideological forces in this wider European, or global context.

We are all delighted that after so many years of profound doubt, Professor Habermas has finally discovered that the West has something positive to offer. We have learnt here that this is a change to be welcomed. At the same time, however, Professor Habermas' conversion to the West has not prevented him from hurling a terrible accusation at the 'gang of four'*: theirs is a NATO-philosophy. Leaving aside the values embraced by the West, the strategic basis of the West happens to be the NATO alliance, whether the Professor likes it or not. I doubt that Western values would survive without this economic and strategic foundation. But it seems that you can have it both ways after all, that you can be for and against the West, whichever is more convenient. The squaring of the circle has finally been achieved by Jürgen Habermas, and I congratulate the Western world on this achievement. Or was it merely an argument to reinforce the accusation that people who write in the *Frankfurter Allgemeine Zeitung*, who believe that one should do more for Europe and NATO and who are in favour of a market economy, are in fact secretly backward-looking, reactionary, apologetic right-wingers? I believe neo-conservative is the modern term.

Ralf Dahrendorf has referred to a country in the heart of Europe,

---

* He meant Andreas Willgruber, Joachim Fest, Michael Sturmer and Wolf Jobst Siedler. See p.80.

but I can't find it on the political map. I am under the impression that one of the worries of our friends and certainly one of my worries is that the Greens are opposed to NATO, that they are largely opposed to the market economy and that they support a form of anti-Americanism that claims that European civilization is being colonized by the United States. It is not only the Greens who argue thus. You can find these arguments in the writings of other politicians as well.

I had always thought that the Western debate over the last five years was concerned primarily with worries about where Germany is going, and especially where it will go, if this kind of anti-Americanism finds political expression not only in the opposition parties but also among the majority of the population. But I now learn that the real problem seems to be the CDU. If the CDU has any merits, then these lie in it being the pro-European and pro-NATO party from 1945 to the present day. I may be too far away from the corridors of power, but as far as I know even the present government has done a great deal in this direction, including sacrificing an important part of our nuclear security on the altars of Atlantic solidarity. So far it has also tried to be more European than some other European countries. How, then, is it possible to claim that the CDU is becoming nationalist if this government is continually being frustrated in its European aspirations not only by its French friends but also by the British? Suffice it to mention European *Ostpolitik*, the EPC or the EMS.

With the possible exception of a lunatic fringe there is no anti-European movement in Germany. Nevertheless, de Gaulle rightly argued that it is an illusion to hope to build Europe by merging the various nations into a faceless entity. The British have never entertained this idea, nor have the French honoured it with the slightest consideration; it is, however, essential to have political entities that are predictable. A political entity called Germany, which knows nothing about its history and only has a selective view of what happened before 1945, cannot be predictable. If I were British or French and I saw Germans engaging in this kind of debate, throwing bits and pieces from the Nazi past at each others' heads and not giving the pre-Nazi period or the post-Nazi period any real thought, I would ask myself how predictable that nation is. Can you risk staking your future, including nuclear security, on that kind of a European system? The issues of the historians' debate and the debate about the past and the future are closely linked with Germany's long-term objectives. Does the

Federal Republic want to play a key role in Europe and in East-West relations? That is not for historians to decide. But our job is to ask questions like: Where do we come from? What has shaped the present? What are the determining factors for the future? There are many different answers, and in a free country different answers are legitimate. Some answers concentrate more on social structures, in short, those of the Bielefeld School. Other answers deal more with the broad cultural background; I should opt for that method. But there are more questions: international relations for example. Knowledge about these considerations enriches our understanding of the past and the present. To reduce German history to just that one dreadful catastrophe, to impose one and only one explanation while shutting ourselves off to any other considerations has a ring of totalitarianism.

In this context I would like to point out that most, if not all of the important books on the Nazi period have been written by people outside the historical profession. We have heard high-flying appeals as to what ought to be done and what should be written. But who has over the past thirty years prevented some of my learned friends in this room from writing the very books that they are now calling for? The same school of thought that keeps saying that the Nazi period is really their prime concern has not produced much worth mentioning, let alone the comprehensive view we would all be keen to read.

We will never get away from the shadow of our recent past. At the same time there is more to German history than the rise and fall of Hitler. It is not just a one-way street to the breakdown of liberal society. There were many options, there was much interdependence with the rest of Europe. The Federal Republic was not a wicked attempt at restoration. If you look at the constitution, if you look at the whole Western orientation since 1945, then this was an attempt, if ever there was one, of a divided nation to define for itself a new moral foundation. Of course it wasn't perfect, but it is – and remains – a moral achievement.

LORD DACRE: This debate is really about the relationship between history and political reality in Germany. It has tended to centre on whether Nazism was unique or whether it was in some way comparable with events elsewhere and on the problem of the search for a new or recovered German identity. I think it's impossible and indeed it would be improper for an English historian to say much about the problem of identity. It is not our problem. As far as comparability is concerned matters used to be pretty simple. There is not a single element in Nazism for which a parallel is not to be found outside Germany in the histories of other countries. What is unique is the amalgam into which these various ideas and programmes were forced in Germany. It was only Germany that converted into action what elsewhere remained mere rhetoric.

How was this possible? If one looks at it historically one must see that what in other countries was a fringe movement was helped to power by the fact that the German establishment, the German intelligentsia put itself behind Nazism. In looking for reasons I agree to a large extent with Michael Stürmer that the Bolshevik Revolution of 1917 was a major force. Ernst Nolte has made that clear. The other force was of course the trauma of the defeat of 1918 which was not morally, intellectually accepted by the German establishment. These two forces caused the German historical and intellectual establishment to put itself behind Nazism, thinking of course that it could control it.

This was partly made possible (and this is what concerns us as historians) by a particular historical philosophy which, though it suffered subtle but important changes in the course of more than a century, had outwardly been more or less continuous since 1830. Ranke, Droysen and Meinecke were the main exponents of this philosophy which was not discredited by the defeat of 1918. The German intelligentsia clung to this philosophy throughout the First World War, one need only read the speeches and articles written by people like Meinecke and Wilamowitz-Moellendorff, and it persisted throughout the Third Reich. Meinecke's letters written during the time of German triumph in 1940 show that he was solidly behind the Nazi war of conquest however much he disapproved of the vulgarity, the cruelty and the anti-intellectualism of Nazism.

As Ranke said, this historical philosophy goes back to the reaction against the French Revolution. It remained continuous until 1945 when it was totally discredited because the amalgam of Nazism was broken up and the amalgam of the historical philosophy which had justified it and made it appear to be part of the continuing German tradition had been destroyed. It is a chastening thought that this historical philosophy would – if Hitler had won the war, which at various points he very nearly did – have been confirmed as the historical orthodoxy in Germany now. We can't say what vengeance Europe might have taken in the forty years following such a German victory but it would have been confirmed by experience. By the mere fact of defeat it was dissolved and is no longer viable.

What has to be done if a new historical philosophy is to be created, a new identity is to be formed around it, has to be done by disintegrating the elements which were forced together into that intellectual and political amalgam which made Nazism possible.

LORD ANNAN: I just want to add a footnote to what Joachim Fest said when he described how he felt about the publication of Nolte's article. Of course there are things which are politically so sensitive that we feel that they should be left unsaid. Some years ago, for example, the Directors of the National Theatre overruled Laurence Olivier and declined to put on Rolf Hochhuth's play *Soldaten* which suggests that Churchill was responsible for the death of General Sikorski. More recently in London the management of the Royal Court Theatre was going to put on a play suggesting that certain Zionist Jews in Hungary had betrayed thousands and thousands of other Jews in order that they themselves might be allowed to escape with Nazi connivance to Israel. Once again pressure was brought to bear and the play was withdrawn. In both cases there were those who thought this intervention was wrong. They thought so because for them television and the theatre live by freedom of expression and no one should be permitted to contradict or censor authors who want to say something however much that something horrifies others.

I have reservations about television and I dislike 'factoid' dramas where the playwright feels free to traduce the reputation of those recently dead. But many great dramatists, Shakespeare himself, took liberties with the facts. And when it comes to the written word I am in no doubt that the general rule must always be to publish. Nolte's article may have been sinister, even malevolent, but we have had a great example of an informed debate, of great heart-searching and of a profound examination of the nature of Germany's past and present. This seems to me a superb thing to have happened. And if it did betray the fact that some new canker is growing in Germany, how much better to allow it to be exposed and indeed be cut out. Of course one must always bear in mind the factor of delicacy in these matters. In 1985 on the occasion of the celebrations of the end of the war forty years earlier there was a television programme in which a Russian, a Frenchman, an Italian, a German and an Englishman were brought together to say what they thought about the war. The programme was moderated by Robert Kee, one of our most powerful television interrogators. He was a bomber pilot during the war, was shot down over Germany and made a prisoner of war for at least three years. Having discussed all the German atrocities Kee turned to the German, Axel von dem Bussche, at the end of the programme and asked him what he thought of the bombing of Dresden. Bussche paused for a moment and said: 'I have lived all my life in a glasshouse and therefore I never throw a brick.' It was a reply of great delicacy in a difficult situation and right at that particular moment. I do not think that Nolte's article was so appalling that the only delicate thing would have been to say, 'I'm afraid we can't publish it.' It seems to me to be an extremely good thing that it was published.

It is characteristic of the British that when we have a historic event to commemorate it does not develop into a great intellectual argument, as in the case of *Historikerstreit* in Germany, but turns into ripe farce. We had to face the question of how to celebrate the tercentenary of the 'Glorious Revolution' in 1988 which, after all, did decide that Britain should be governed by rule of law, that the judges should be independent, that the sovereign would be unable to suspend the laws and that no standing army could be kept without consent of parliament. The government decided that this should be commemorated, but once the decision was made it did its very best to reduce the celebrations to a football match conducted against Holland. This is because the authorities are afraid of giving offence to Roman Catholics and particularly Roman Catholics in Northern Ireland where the Battle of the Boyne finally decided that William III should be sovereign of Britain and not James II, regardless of the fact that Roman Catholics benefited as much as Protestants by the rule of law, by an independent judiciary, by no standing army, etc.

CHRISTIAN MEIER: I find it rather touching that the non-Germans should follow our *querelle allemande* so patiently. Michael Stürmer has characterized the vast range of issues we are faced with very well. Listening to all this, I can't help feeling that Germans are apparently not to be trusted. For if so much depends on history, we are unstable partners in the Western alliance and the European community. No matter how we look at these matters, the fact remains that a nation which has done something as dreadful as what the Germans did between 1933 and 1945 can no longer be sure of itself. Once you have done something like this you no longer know what you are capable of. These events will surely not repeat themselves, they can't repeat themselves, but uncertainty remains. We have to ask ourselves how much history, or historical awareness, or even just a feeling of having had a certain history affects the political reliability, the predictability, the actions and the thoughts of a nation.

I would like to come back to our starting point, the historians' dispute. Until the contrary has been proved, I maintain that the editorial staff of *Die Zeit* in Hamburg determined the course of the debate by deciding which historians should take part in it. After the appearance of Habermas' piece in *Die Zeit* which was followed by Joachim Fest's article in the *Frankfurter Allgemeine* a number of historians were asked by *Die Zeit* to contribute and others were not. The debate did not really develop naturally, it did not consist of opinions expressed more or less spontaneously by a series of intellectuals from different backgrounds. Instead we have the strange circumstance of Robert Leicht, political editor of *Die Zeit* in Hamburg, and, to a lesser extent, Joachim Fest in Frankfurt deciding who should take part. It is significant that the dispute met with such a huge response not only in Germany but far beyond. This can surely be explained by the fact that all these German matters are of interest abroad, precisely because other countries know that they must keep an eye on what is going on in Germany, since one never knows if this nation can be trusted.

As far as Germany is concerned, I don't think one can put it as simply as Ralf Dahrendorf did when he said that the *Historikerstreit* is a process of redefining political positions. I agree that it is a factor which has played a certain role, but there are at least two more. One is the shattering of hopes of progress. These hopes had flared up once more after 1968 but with the oil crisis in the early seventies all expectations for the future were stifled the world over. Germany was affected in a special way. As a result of this collapse we tried to escape from our history into the future.

Secondly, I think a change in the international situation, that is to say, in the relations between the superpowers was an important factor which made itself felt in domestic affairs. Thirdly, there is the generation problem. Forty years after the war an overwhelming majority of Germans are too young to have had any part in these events. The oldest of those who no longer had anything to do with Nazism are now almost sixty years old. They are particularly receptive to the issues raised in the course of the historians' dispute. As historians we are tempted to equate our views with those of a whole nation. It is not only a question of knowledge, but of how knowledge is registered. After the war we knew about the extermination of the Jews. Many of us suppressed this knowledge, others did not know how to cope with it. History has shown again and again that it takes a while for people to take in and digest exceptional circumstances, it is not enough just to be aware of them. The Holocaust cannot merely be described as something hitherto unknown simply because it is incomprehensible. It does credit to the human intellect that it refuses to grasp these events. I know of no other event which is as difficult to comprehend. I would say that any normal person should reject the mere thought of trying to understand Hitler, even though it is our duty as historians to do so. In my view the real problem lies in the fact that this crime cannot be fully taken in by any normal mind.

Of course historians are confronted with this problem, but it affects them less because they can start analyzing straightaway. Their task is to enable a wider non-specialist audience to experience history. I don't know how effective the teaching of history in schools is. There are many arguments in favour of promoting the teaching of history in schools and elsewhere, but I wonder to what extent it is possible to tackle the problem of how to deal with our history in this way. The question is, how can a nation with sixty million inhabitants come to terms with this history and, to take up Michael Stürmer's point, to what extent is a certain clarity and a certain acceptance of our past a condition for predictability? As far as I can tell, neither the Germans nor other countries are sufficiently clear yet about themselves, about who they are and what is expected of them. Other countries are fortunate in that they are more firmly embedded in their history and are thus more able to cope with a rough patch.

But what difference does the insecurity about this episode in our history make, what difference does it make that parents did not tell a whole generation of children about what they lived through? Many of my students told me that their parents had remained silent on this subject although these students were not really under the impression that their parents had anything to hide. And yet they chose not to speak because they felt they could deal with these things better by suppressing them. Everyone knows about what the Germans did during those years and we must still bear the responsibility. Leaving the Russians aside, other nations also have something to answer for. But they are not reproached. There is, therefore, a discrepancy between those who must bear the guilt and those who nearly get off scot-free. What difference does it make that our leaders were tried in Nuremberg? It was right that they should be tried but nowhere else were similar crimes condemned after the war. Is that disproportionate? I can think of a number of situations in which the Germans play a very special role. They are not in a position to complain about it. Consciously or subconsciously the Germans ask themselves whether others deserved to be let off so lightly. It also makes them insecure in their relations with others.

In 1953 Brecht advised the Bonn government to swap its people for the East Germans. This is obviously impossible. One can replace governments but not peoples. Each nation reacts to history in an individual and more or less unpredictable way. This is a problem which needs closer examination in order to discover how to deal with it. For practical and realistic reasons I think it is important to accept that the Federal Republic has enjoyed forty years of successful democracy. By careful analysis and by describing the Nazi period historically we should find a *modus vivendi* so that innocent descendants can live with what their grandfathers and fathers did. This will probably take several decades.

I think Michael Stürmer's statement that everything is concentrated on twelve years of German history and not on a millennium rather contradicts his complaint about the fact that Germans aren't writing any books about National Socialism.

MICHAEL STÜRMER: I can't understand that contradiction, that is precisely what I was saying.

CHRISTIAN MEIER: It is true to say that those twelve years are inhibiting. We can no longer see the positive aspects of German history without being aware of the fact that they did not prevent us from doing what we did in the years from 1933 to 1945.

CHARLES MAIER: I seem to be condemned continually to misread Michael Stürmer, so perhaps I should stop trying. I would like to make a point about identity and predictability in history. Although Karl Dietrich Bracher is a political scientist he has, perhaps by methodological affiliation, done worthy work on the twelve years of Nazism. I don't see many of us reading 1945 as a restoration. This was a trope of neo-Marxist interpretations of the late sixties and early seventies.

MICHAEL STÜRMER: 'Second restoration' was one of the headlines that were used again and again in connection with the historians' debate.

CHARLES MAIER: I don't know who gets put in the headlines.

MICHAEL STÜRMER: Politicians, historians.

CHARLES MAIER: Let me speak a little more generally. How does the question Michael Stürmer raised about the trauma of the Bolshevik Revolution relate to the Final Solution? I certainly believe in comparative history. The trauma of the Bolshevik Revolution and the fear that it would overtake Central and even Western Europe was experienced by many. But they did not all conclude that fascism was the only answer. Professor Nolte's tendency to over-generalize worries me. This idea that the Industrial Revolution explains every subsequent ideology, that some large historical complex in the relatively distant past is responsible for the present is an example of this.

It is the task of the historian to follow the *different* paths which lead from any particular trauma in the past and take us to the present. It was clear to many Western liberals and Marxists at the time that the Spanish civil war was a catastrophe. But when we look at the Spanish transition to democracy now we can observe that the Civil War experience has been used as a buttress of consensus by a country which is finding a way of preserving centrist politics. One cannot simply cite past traumas as explanatory causes for every outcome. It is not a historical way of proceeding. This method has however been used in some of the rhetoric of the *Historikerstreit*.

Predictability in international politics does not depend on a knowledge of history or a feeling of identity. As an actor in the international arena Germany was not predictable at the time of the Weimar Republic. The Italians were certainly not predictable towards the end of the 1930s. Some people are now making a career out of saying that the Americans were not predictable in the late 1980s. We may not be, but we have been predictable for a few years and we probably will be for the next few years. In any case predictability does not depend on our having historical self-knowledge or not. People only talk about identity when they don't have it. I am not really concerned about the Germans discovering their identity.

I agree that Habermas' agenda is inconsistent. I don't see how he can express both scepticism about NATO and a commitment to the West. I believe predictability means commitment to certain moral values and not to a view of history. Professor Habermas seems to have that commitment to values these days. I still don't agree that history can exhaust identity. There are elements of national behaviour which must be explained by other disciplines, even though I love to think of history as a *via maesta* of scholarship. Identity is not the only problem for international behaviour and the citation of past events is not really the historian's way of explaining it.

MICHAEL STÜRMER: What Charles Maier said is very interesting but I only agree with him to a limited degree about the link between historical images, politics and predictability. He said this was not relevant in Weimar. I disagree entirely. As far as Weimar is concerned there is a historical image based on 1848: black, red, gold. There is another based on 1871: black, white, red. The third image based on 1917 is red and the fourth image is the revolution to end all revolutions. Everyone thought they could use the latter image in some way but it overwhelmed them all. That should teach us how complex and important images are. We know today that historians of the Weimar period have, on the whole, propagated the wrong image, mostly the one of 1870. There were some, however, who were ambiguous, and others who were fascinated by 1848, but by the time their books came out the Weimar Republic had already been exhausted as a subject. But the internal debate in the Weimar period was about colours, images and power.

WOLFGANG MOMMSEN: I would like to reply to Michael Stürmer and comment on what Lord Dacre said. I do not agree with Charles Maier on the issue of national identity. Values in a political context always have a historical base. In fact, if there is a real issue in this debate it is the question of how the historical base of West German democracy and its fundamental values should be delineated. The liberal-democratic paradigm established in the 1950s is no longer accepted *prima facie*. It is being questioned, and possible alternative positions are gradually emerging. We should really be more concerned with the mentality of the general public and not so much with what professional historians think. Unfortunately we know very little in this field, but historians tend to react to what they think the public wants or to what the public thinks.

By and large Lord Dacre's description of a long-term tradition of historical thought which we tend to identify with historicism is accurate. I see what has happened in the last few years as an attempt to return towards historicist or neo-historicist positions. Stürmer, Hildebrandt, Hagen Schulze and several others keep presenting explanatory models which can clearly be located in the nineteenth century. The *Mittellage* argument, for example, is typically neo-Rankian. To put it crudely, I think that Wilhelminian interpretations of German history are creeping in again and are being used to explain why things went wrong, not so much in terms of a deficit in liberal values and structures, but rather in terms of objective factors like Germany's position in the centre of Europe. I am sceptical as to whether this is a plausible way of explaining anything. But it has a function. It provides a basis for an interpretation of history which certainly cannot be described as liberal. I don't want to go into whether this is justified, I am just describing this phenomenon.

We went through a phase in the Federal Republic when German history was 'out', when everybody went in for European history. Now, all of a sudden, we are faced with a search for German national identity; it is not clear, however, whether the subject of this identity should be the West Germans alone, the West Germans and the Germans in the GDR, or perhaps a German cultural nation in its entirety. It has become more obvious than ever that the Nazi period stands in the way of reconstructing a notion of German national history which could provide the basis for a decent image of the German past. Is the National Socialist period an aberration from the normal path of redevelopment which does not really belong to German history, or did it grow out of a trend in German history? The issue is an old one, but German historians are now coming up with different answers. Andreas Hillgruber has discovered Prussia as the key to the problem of how to defend Central Europe against Bolshevism and he has put the blame for the destruction of Prussia on Great Britain in particular. These are new tones which I, as a historian of historiography, could also describe as old tones. These things keep recurring.

Similarly, I am irritated by attempts to explain recent German history in terms of the trauma of 1917, the trauma of Bolshevism. The German bourgeoisie was not really endangered by Bolshevism at any stage except possibly after 1945, but it is still the stock-in-trade argument used to explain why the German middle classes voted for the National Socialists. I think we need much more sophisticated answers which cannot be used as a cover-up for what went wrong with German history.

I admit, it is very difficult to quote Michael Stürmer because he can be quoted in so many different ways. I am sorry to say that he appears to argue that we ought to create a consensus about German history which should on the whole be positive rather than negative. Nolte has stated that we must fight 'anti-national' notions of German history. I think other nations have reason to worry about this; it could mean what I described as the reconstruction of a 'German' concept of German history along traditional lines. I know it is foolish to say one must no longer write exclusively German history, however, German history ought to be written in a way that differs completely from the old-fashioned approach.

We should freely admit that something went wrong with Germany's history. We started afresh in 1945, or, say, in the 1950s. There is a trend in the Federal Republic supported by some historians, sometimes innocently, not to recognize the fact that there was a fundamental break in the development of German historical consciousness in conjunction with the founding of the Federal Republic, a democratic state closely associated with the West and its political values. This is what we quarrel about. It is a vital issue because in some ways the identity of the Federal Republic is based upon a negation of parts of Germany's recent past. That affects the position of Germany in the world. It is interesting, Herr Stürmer, that we share the same goal in that we want to make sure that West Germany is part of the Western world and remains integrated into Western political culture. We seem, however, to come up with different recipes as to how to rewrite German history in order to achieve this objective. I think that some of those who cling to the idea that one should create a new and less negative image of German history were quite frightened to see what impact this message can have on the general public. We have been talking about the *Historikerstreit* in the past tense, but I think this is wrong. The dispute will go on probably for the next five, six, seven years for reasons which have nothing to do with the historical profession, but rather with the political mentality of the Germans in both Germanies.

RALF DAHRENDORF: I think we might have spoken about the position of the GDR on this issue. Several speakers have alluded to it. After all, we are discussing German history and not the history of the Federal Republic. It would be interesting to discover to what extent this debate is only taking place in the Federal Republic or whether it is looming under the surface or even in the open in the GDR. How does the official position of the GDR relate to this soul-searching about history and identity? But first I suggest we broaden the scope by listening to Robert Conquest.

ROBERT CONQUEST: I do not want to deal with the question of national identity which has been discussed at great length in the German context. It is a notoriously complex and ambiguous issue in the Soviet Union. Still, I would like to note the current revival in the Soviet Union of a virulent type of anti-semitic Russian nationalism, even penetrating the party. In my view it presents one of the possible Soviet futures and perhaps as likely a one as democratization.

I think we all accept the proposition that the Nazi crimes were unique and uniquely horrible, that they were a reaction against the communist terrors seems to be untenable. It is conceivable that *support* for the National Socialists may largely have come as a reaction to Lenin's international civil war launched in 1918, but the actual crimes of the Holocaust are of a totally different nature from Stalin's crimes and I see no connection whatever. But although there is no causative connection, comparisons can still be made.

Outside the German context one is not perhaps quite as 'Hitler-ocentric' about these matters. I recently spoke to a Jewish emigré from Russia, a scholar, who, though not a historian, has been following the German dispute. He referred to the argument raised again and again, that by comparing Hitler with Stalin, one was excusing Hitler. And he pointed out, that if, on the other hand, one said that Hitler was a thousand times worse than Stalin, one was excusing Stalin. For a Russian, Stalin simply looms bigger than Hitler and of course it must be remembered that Stalin is not yet among the dead. If we agree that the Nazi crimes were nevertheless worse, did the two systems have a central point in common and if so, what was it? I tend to agree with Hugh Seton

Watson, who says that what National Socialism and Stalinism had in common was a moral nihilism. Though each took different forms and chose different victims, they did share that particular characteristic. In that sense therefore they were of a type which put them apart from other atrocities in the past.

The first attempt by the non-Nazi world to come to grips with Hitlerism was in a sense thwarted by the Soviet presence at Nuremberg. It seems anomalous that one of the states passing judgement over Nazi Germany, as an aggressor should itself have been expelled from the League of Nations six years previously on that charge. The mere fact that the Soviet judge Nikitchenko had been a judge in the faked Zinoviev trial and other falsified cases made nonsense of Nuremberg. One of the Soviet prosecutors, Lev Sheinin, had furthermore been head of the prosecution 'Section Investigating Important Cases' in Moscow, and had been responsible in one way or another for almost all the main frame ups: his name actually appears in a number of them. So there was a direct link with the Stalin terror which in a sense prevented proper judgement over Hitler. Then the Katyn massacre was of course one of the charges at Nuremberg, although not mentioned in the verdict. That issue has become topical. Recently a member of the Polish Communist apparat stated on Warsaw television that many Poles believed the Russians were responsible. If war criminals are still being prosecuted, there are no doubt those among the perpetrators of Katyn who are still alive. These Nuremberg issues are perhaps not central to our theme: but they surely valuate some of our problems.

In studying Stalin's terror we are handicapped in a way which historians of Germany are not. For a long time we did not have access to many of the real facts and figures and only managed to glean some of them with difficulty. That is partly due to the census of 1937 which resulted in the Census Board being shot and substituted by a new one. Nevertheless we have been able to obtain roughly the numbers involved. They are on a very large scale. For example, when I wrote my book *Harvest of Sorrow* about the first phase of the Stalin terrors in the early thirties I had not seen an obscure article by V. P. Danilov, the leading Soviet expert on the collectivization. In it he says the population deficit from 1930 to January 1937 was 15–16 million. That includes unborn babies. But even without them the death figure cannot be much lower than about eleven million, to which should be added not fewer than three million peasants in labour camps in 1937, and dying there later.

It has been claimed that the Kulak deportations were just that – 'deportations'. They were not. Whole families were removed to areas of the Arctic, where they were just dumped in the Taiga and Tundra. Several million, mainly children, perished. It is not possible to say how many died in what year, but it was probably something like three million in the first two or three years and more later. This was a terror operation. It was not designed to kill every Kulak on the spot. But it was designed to destroy what was regarded as a hostile category. The same applies to the second operation, the terror famine of 1932–3, which was limited to certain areas. Food was taken away and when there was none left, there was no relief. During the third wave of terror in 1937–8, which was followed up later, about eight million people were taken to prisons or executed.

There was torture on a huge scale. (It is interesting that the Central Committee decree of January 1939 authorizing torture, justified it by stating that the bourgeois intelligence services had always used it.) But the most striking characteristic of these terrors – and I think it distinguishes it from the German atrocities in various ways – is the falsification. Not that the Nazis didn't falsify. But the style of Soviet falsification was an integral part of the terror at every level. Every accusation was false. There was, according to Stalin's propaganda, a huge conspiracy based on Trotsky and Hitler. In the long run, millions of people were involved in it and compelled to confess. It was an enormous and unprecedented falsification.

However, looking at it from a historian's point of view, it is also true that Stalin never totally committed himself to given actions. He played his cards very close to his chest and did not give openings to his critics. As I said, he did not kill all the Kulaks. When he was conducting his anti-semitic campaign in 1952–3, some of the doctors in the 'Doctors' Plot' were gentiles, so it could be seen as not anti-semitic. In the same way the famine of 1932–3 was simply treated as non-existent. This helped to deceive Westerners, starting of course with Sidney and Beatrice Webb, whose book accurately describes the Soviet Union as it was on paper but is entirely wrong about the country as it was in practice. This tendency has survived.

I want to point out certain similarities between the Stalin and Hitler terrors. In spite of all the differences they are in some respects perhaps more alike than we realize. If we go back to the Kulaks, there are some curious parallels. Stalin did not order the physical extermination of the whole category, nor did he obtain it. But he did have a kind of mystical definition of what a Kulak was. You could, for example, become a Kulak by employing labour or having more horses than other people, but you could not cease to be one by getting rid of them. You were then considered to be concealing your 'essence'. A Kulak was cut off from decent society, whatever he did. Of course this also applied to his children. The son of a Kulak had 'Kulak son' on his identity card and could not get a job in the cities. It was a special category which you entered into, as it were, hereditarily. In a certain sense this went back to the beginning of the Revolution. In *Cancer Ward* there is a man who worked all his life. When he is called a bourgeois, he bursts out, saying, 'what do you mean, I'm bourgeois, I've worked all my life, even though my father was a merchant class 3', and they reply, in effect, 'Yes, that's it, you're a bourgeois.' So there is that type of parallel.

But the most extraordinary parallel in this context was drawn by Vassily Grossman, the great Jewish Soviet novelist, whose own mother died in the gas chambers. He was the author of the great documentary book on Treblinka, *The Hell of Treblinka*, and was joint editor with Ilya Ehrenberg of the Soviet section of the *Black Book* on the Nazi Holocaust, never published in the Soviet Union. When he writes of the Ukrainian terror famine and the Kulak deportations, he makes a direct comparison with the Third Reich by stating: 'Just as the Germans proclaim, the Jews are not human beings. Thus did Lenin and Stalin proclaim, Kulaks are not human beings.' He repeats this theme on several occasions. Grossman points out that the children dying of starvation look just like the children in the Nazi gas chambers. 'These were', he writes, 'Soviet children and those who were putting them to death were Soviet people.' In his last novel, *Life and Fate*, Grossman even lets the Jewish hero Shtrum, a physicist, say, 'To me a distinction based on social origin seems legitimate and moral. But Germans obviously consider a distinction based on nationality to be equally moral. We have the same principle.' That is going rather far, you might say, but that is how it appeared to a prominent Soviet and Jewish figure, although he may be overstressing the point precisely because less was known about the Soviet past.

Nowadays we do all have a general idea of the Soviet past and the Stalin terror. The central question however is, what is happening about coming to grips with it? Is anything comparable to what German historians have done in dealing with Nazi history taking place in the Soviet Union? One of the problems of course is that the same party is still in power. This obviously creates obstacles. There are individuals who might have difficulties with a total rewriting, a true revision of history. The first attempt was made in 1956, in Khrushchev's time, and died out in 1965. A great deal was said in certain rather limited areas. At the time this was sometimes referred to as de-Stalinization. A Soviet dissident pointed out that de-Nazification involved 90,000 people being put through the tribunals in Germany, whilst in the Soviet Union it was a matter of a few dozen secret policemen who had come out of the political struggle on the wrong side.

After Khrushchev's attempt to bring part of history back to light had failed, there followed a curious period, which lasted twenty years. During that time the whole attitude to history was anomalous in the most scandalous intellectual fashion. It shook the Soviet intelligentsia. They hated and hate this attitude (and now they say so). There was no official story about the terror. In Stalin's time the official line was that a large conspiracy of Trotskyites and Fascists had been discovered, that some of those incriminated had been tried by courts, had confessed and been rightly sentenced, whilst others, not many, had been sent to labour camps. A perfectly clear story, which is totally untrue.

After 1965–6 some of the people from the great trials were rehabilitated, others were not, but nothing whatever was said, there was no official story, true or false, about the trials themselves, which formed the central political actions in the years from 1936–8. There were odd penetrations. Bukharin and Rykov were briefly acknowledged not to have been spies and terrorists at a small historical conference. But it did not last, and Bukharin's son and widow tried for years to get him rehabilitated. They succeeded only in 1987–8.

Glasnost has brought to light an enormous amount of material on social and economic horrors, some of which is extraordinary. A year or two ago no Minister of Health would have stated in a public speech that his nation ranked fiftieth in infant mortality, after the United Arab Emirates. Horrible reports about hospitals, about unemployment, about homelessness are being revealed. The Soviets are being informed about such things. This was the main area first affected by glasnost. History came later.

But now it is official policy that the facts must not be concealed.

Gorbachev himself has stated that the actions of 1937–8 are to be blamed on those then in power. General statements of that kind have been made. But official historical journals like *Voprosy istorii* ('Questions of History') stood pat on the old stories until 1988. The odd items cropped up in other papers. I found a rehabilitation of Muralov, one of those shot in the Piatakov trial of January 1937, none of whom had previously been rehabilitated. But that was in an odd corner of 'Socialist Industry', because Muralov was an industrialist. There were occasional articles in *Izvestiya* making a few general points at great length, implying the trials were faked. A long article on Raskolnikov, one of the few leading Bolsheviks to defect in the late thirties, was printed. He wrote an open letter to Stalin, which has always been described as fascist. Much of it was published in *Ogonyok* in 1987, and contained references to the trials. (Raskolnikov had been rehabilitated in the early sixties and posthumously restored to party membership, but in the seventies this was countermanded and he was de-rehabilitated and re-expelled. His fate shows that history does not necessarily move forward. The reverse can be the case.)

Serious reassessment on the historical side at first took place at closed, but not specially secret, meetings. The *Christian Science Monitor* in mid-1987 reported a conversation on tape, when N. Shmelyov, the economist, is quoted as saying that 17 million people went through the Gulag. It was claimed that this is a well-known figure. Furthermore Shmelyov stated that in 1940 the population in the dreadful arctic camps of Kolyma was over three million; and that five million families were deported in the Kulak period. And so on. The interesting thing about this particular statement was that Shmelyov was arguing on economic grounds. The attack on Stalinism was being conducted on the grounds that Stalin's method of running the economy was disastrous. So Shmelyov is not taking a humanitarian view. He is asking what those 17 million in the camps gave to the nation: two canals, one of which did not work, and a few logs from the north which could have been better obtained by free labour. This is an odd approach. It makes it possible to point out to the leadership that in order to get the economy going, the Stalinist myth must be destroyed, and to argue that as long as Stalinist economists and supporters of his method are left in charge, the country will ruin itself. This opens the opportunity for attack on historical issues as well. History was thus brought in as a pragmatic ploy without any regard to the humanitarian aspect. Later the issues of humanitarianism and of truth for its own sake began to break through and increasingly so.

There is an interesting historical point linking this with the Nazi period. On a recent visit to Moscow a friend of mine was talking to the head of a history institute about diplomatic history before the war. He revealed that there was not a single student anywhere in the Soviet Union working on the period 1939–41. That is a rather remarkable gap. However the pressure to reveal more is increasing. The Poles are now asking for an examination of that period, and one of the demands of the Latvian demonstrators, who drew attention to themselves recently, was that the secret protocols of the Nazi-Soviet pact be published. It is obvious why students would not choose to work on this subject a few years ago. They were not likely to get much promotion from it. Even so, it is a little odd that no one was doing it at all. In mid-1987 a young archivist made a speech in which he revealed that he had been personally extracting information from the files of the Supreme Court archives. He had managed to list on index cards the names of 86,000 people who had been shot by order of the Supreme Court – a very small proportion of the total. In the course of doing this he had discovered a number of previously unknown details about the fate of certain individuals. We now learn that the archives of many of the courts are being destroyed, presumably in anticipation of further glasnost. Quite a lot seemed to have been done away with in the sixties and seventies. It is said that several million files have disappeared. The archives of the Supreme Court and its Military Collegium, the body to which Nikitchenko belonged and which was responsible for the public trials, are in question. There are orders to dispose of about 15,000 cases a week. 1940 has already been covered as has 1948–9 and they plan to deal with the lot by 1992. The official argument was that they were disposing of the files owing to lack of space. This became an issue, the first purely historiographical issue in the Soviet Union. The new semi-underground paper, *Glasnost*, later repressed, raised it as a matter of concern to historians all over the world. It has been suggested that we should offer these documents house care. At any rate Western historians have an interest in this matter and something should be done.

If glasnost does continue, and if, as I think is possible, Gorbachev feels he has to use it as an issue to fight on, as Khruschev did, the anti-Stalin issue, then we may get discussions about the past of the kind which have preoccupied German historians. In part Soviet historians are raring to go, but of course in part they are not. There are numbers of articles by prominent historians saying they do not want to cast dirt on their past. That line has been strongly supported by some in the Politburo. Meanwhile editors of more progressive papers like *Moscow News* are printing what they can, while they can. There is an air of pessimism around, a belief that one cannot be sure of anything, that we will get more information, but we may not get full disclosures; and that it may not persist. Even so, the notion that we do not have enough material to know what was going on has already proved to be untrue. We do know what was going on. Though information is not so lavishly available as in other countries, there is now enough and more than enough material for us to form a clear judgement of the Stalin period.

SAMUEL ETTINGER: Robert Conquest's admirable report presents a true picture of some of the most awful aspects of the Soviet regime. Numerically more people may have been killed during the Soviet terror than under the Nazi regime, but nonetheless there are great differences even between those elements which Nazism and Bolshevism appear to have in common. One common element is the rejection of Western culture, Western ideas and institutions. Both regimes regarded Western influences, especially democracy, as inimical and presented their national revolutions as the best moral and social answer to the 'rotten West'. The other common aspect is lawlessness. It wasn't an independent judiciary but the will of the ruler which prevailed as the supreme law.

On the other hand there is Hitler's ideology. Hitler developed his ideology in the early stages of his life and pursued it rigorously throughout. Stalin did just the opposite. He was an opportunist from the very beginning. He didn't have ideas and that's the great difference between them. Stalin's only goal was power and he was ready to exploit any situation to attain it. Therefore he imagined that he was surrounded by various enemies and, particularly in the last stages of his life, he became paranoid and killed people left and right. But he was not really ideological at all and German historians like Nolte and also Fest are wrong to suggest that there is a similarity between *Rassenkampf* and *Klassenkampf*, racial and class conflict. The Bolsheviks began at an early stage to use bourgeois specialists in various fields of the economy and in the army. The basic attitude was, if a bourgeois could be useful then he was used, if one was afraid of him and felt one needed to do something about him, then he was disposed of.

I must disagree even more firmly with Robert Conquest on another point. Social origin was a major issue after the Revolution but this policy was more or less abandoned in 1932–3 when industrial developments began and Stalin needed manpower. From 1934 onwards social origin is hardly mentioned any more, and a man who worked at 'building socialism' became free of his hereditary disease.

ROBERT CONQUEST: I don't think that is correct. The difference between the ideologies is very important. Race theory differs from class theory. It involves killing all members of a racial group whereas class theory doesn't necessarily imply the equivalent. I don't think it the least true that Stalin was not ideological. Collectivization was done on ideological (if to some extent also disciplinary) grounds, to get rid of a petit bourgeois class, as one could not achieve socialism while the free peasantry existed. It was done against all the natural tendencies of the economy, for ideological reasons; and it isn't true that they allowed people of the wrong class to take jobs. (Of course they used individuals; they weren't so rigorous about this division that they could not be pragmatic at times: Lenin was himself of course a bourgeois.) But the Kulaks were forbidden to take jobs in the cities. They did sneak in but when they were found they were thrown out.

I think you are perhaps thinking of 1940 when people like Malenkov started saying that one should no longer worry so much about origin. There was also an intermediate period up to 1931–2 when they used bourgeois specialists, but then they got rid of them. There were innumerable trials of bourgeois specialists. By that time the regime had educated its own communist specialists and although it was not entirely non-tactical on this either, *grosso modo* it destroyed the old intelligentsia on class, i.e. on ideological grounds. Only later, when the place was *kulakrein*, as one might say, when only grandchildren existed, was the theory that they could not be assimilated abandoned.

SAMUEL ETTINGER: We have a real point of disagreement here. I don't see the struggle against the Kulaks as an ideological one. It was political. Stalin was afraid that a large sector of the population would not agree to a communist regime. Therefore he aimed at destroying their economic basis. This was done for political reasons. The communists also wanted to buy the poor peasants by taking possessions from richer peasants and giving them partly to the poorer ones. This is not ideology, it's pure and simple tactics in politics and economics.

I also disagree about the Kulaks. They were not persecuted on ideological grounds. It's true that they were not allowed to live in the cities, many others were not allowed to live in the cities, again for practical reasons. The cities grew so much in a very short period that some checks were necessary. Various excuses were therefore sought to control the population influx. We should also look at the settlement policy in the vast territories outside central Russia, which was pursued not only by the communists but had already been applied by the Tsarist regime. There is an admirable chapter in Carr's history of the Russian Revolution about this policy under the Tsars and under Soviet rule. Manpower was needed not only for industrial construction but for settlement in Siberia, Kasakhstan and other places. The Kulaks were the reserve for this.

It is wrong to speak about extermination. The Bolsheviks didn't want to exterminate the Kulaks, they wanted to use them as slaves. The Bolsheviks didn't think this up themselves. Slave labour has been an important element in Russian history for generations. There was an interlude beginning with the great reforms of Alexander II and lasting until the end of the nineteenth or the beginning of the twentieth century, but then slave labour again became a means to achieve economic ends. To compare the extermination of Jews and Gypsies by the Nazis with the persecution and expulsion – not extermination – of the Kulaks is incorrect. Then there is another difference: why did they set up all those show trials for millions, why should they need confessions if they could just as well shoot people without them confessing? Because they wanted to offer some kind of explanation in rational terms for the general population. The inhabitants of the ghettos in Eastern or Central Europe were not even given a show trial. They were simply exterminated. Again there is the specific Soviet attitude to opposition groups, to opposing ideologies. The surest sign of opportunism is the readiness to co-operate with opposite ideologies. I have already mentioned Rapallo and the military co-operation with the Germans. As from the second half of the 1930s Stalin continually sought a rapprochement with Hitler. He achieved it in 1939. If ideology had been so important to him, he would not have pursued such a policy so eagerly.

ROBERT CONQUEST: But then Hitler achieved this too. You are saying he is more ideological and he should not have achieved it?

SAMUEL ETTINGER: Yes I am, despite the fact that Hitler was also pragmatic at times. If the Western powers had strongly resisted the persecution of the Jews, Hitler would not have dared to execute them so ruthlessly. It was only after his great successes, when he realized no one cared about the Jews, that he decided to put his ideology into practice. Stalin, on the other hand, actually co-operated with the Nazis to destroy the democratic regime of Weimar. However, in the early thirties, he began to be afraid of the success of the Nazis and adopted the policy of the 'united front' with some liberal and social democratic forces. From 1936 onwards he abandoned it and co-operated with Hitler again. This is sheer opportunism.

I am the last person to defend Stalin's crimes. I have devoted a great part of my scholarly life to the study of the history of Soviet Jewry, to understanding the situation of Soviet Jews and looking into the persecution and discrimination they suffered from the second half of the thirties. But if we fail to see the difference between Stalin's and Hitler's regime we are in no position to understand the internal development of Soviet and German society.

Despite my admiration for Vasily Grossman and Solzhenitsyn, their novels are hardly historical documents. If we cannot piece the various facts together to create a mosaic, a picture of the situation, we are unable to explain it. We cannot form moral judgements until we have studied the historical facts properly.

NORMAN STONE: We are not going to find a common ground on a question like this. Robert Conquest didn't mention the line taken by many Ukrainians who see the famine of 1930–1 as a deliberate attempt at genocide by the Soviet Union. I can't see how one can say anything really meaningful about all that. In the end it can't be proved.

I want to pick a certain amount of disagreement with Professor Ettinger. One should never quite believe the attempts to rationalize totalitarian regimes and the propaganda involved. After 1945, during the Nuremberg trials, the men and women who had had a part in running Auschwitz made the point, and I have no doubt that there was a certain amount of, I won't say truth, but at least verisimilitude in it, that they had to put people in camps because otherwise typhoid might have broken out and the authorities would have had a terrible administrative problem on their hands. The same sort of rationalization can no doubt be, and has been made for the disorganization of Soviet agriculture in the years of the first five-year plan.

There is a point of the greatest interest in the discussion of Russian history. It is an argument which can be applied much more clearly to Russia than ever it can to Germany. Are we to say that Russian history is condemned because of what happened in the twenties and thirties, that there is a development leading to Bolshevism, which in its turn leads to Stalin, that there is a long history of slave labour and exploitation of the peasants? Are we to look at Soviet history and say it inevitably leads to Stalinism, that this is a country which did not have the Renaissance, the Reformation? I would like to make the point that another Russia was developing before 1914. If one added up the figures one would probably discover that more people were executed in England between 1860 and 1914 than were executed in Russia in that period. The death penalty for instance was abolished in Russia in the 1860s and was only reintroduced in 1881 by exceptional legislation as a response to the first wave of terrorist agitation following the 'Land and Liberty' revolt after which military tribunals were brought in. In the 1880s there were altogether 7000 policemen, 2000 of whom were in St Petersburg. If we are dealing with a tyrannical state at all, it has fewer bureaucrats, far fewer policemen than the Third Republic. There is a serious point to be made here. The horrors of what happened in Russia in the twenties and thirties can be ascribed to communism. It has, after all, produced the same phenomena in China, Cambodia and in large parts of Eastern Europe, admittedly only for a few years. We are dealing here with an ideology which is imposed more or less from outside and should not be taken as a comment on the nature of the country's history. This is the point which ought to be made when talking about German history in comparison.

JÜRGEN KOCKA: Three brief comments on Robert Conquest's paper which I found most informative. I was pleased that Conquest stressed that he couldn't see any evidence for interpreting the Nazi Holocaust as a reaction to what happened in the Soviet

Union either between 1917 and 1919 or later in the thirties. I don't think there is any evidence for this, and if participants could distance themselves from this speculative argument the debate would become more rational and less heated.

I am not really competent to contribute to the controversy about similarities and differences between the deportation of the Kulaks and the mass murder of the Jews. I am, however, struck by the discrepancy between the different figures and interpretations one reads in the literature on the famine. A German periodical recently published research results putting the number of deaths caused by the deportations between 1930 and 1932 at 300,000. How sure can we be about the interpretation of the famine of 1932–5? Was the death of millions a result of compulsive collectivization, the consequence of political actions, or was there a plan to annihilate millions? It seems to me that one must establish which of these options apply in order to be able to judge differences and similarities between Stalin and Hitler, and I wonder what the literature reveals on this point.

I was impressed by Conquest's description of how this catastrophic episode of Soviet history was covered up and not confronted in the Soviet Union for many decades. As he pointed out, this differs strongly from the way in which the Germans have discussed their past. From what Conquest said, I have the impression that this cover-up has not really been a source of strength to the Soviet Union. Some people think that the intensity of the German debate about German history between 1933 and 1945 is a liability which prevents us from having any self-assurance. There is the fear that too much discussion and remembrance of the catastrophic events could render us incapable of collective action, would make us *zukunftsunfähig*. In the light of the Soviet example the contrary seems to be the case: the intense discussion of the Nazi period may well have been a source of intellectual, political and moral strength in West Germany.

EBERHARD JÄCKEL: I would like to make a few comments on the German-Soviet comparison and on relations between the two countries. I don't think historians can scientifically establish whether the crimes committed by one side are worse than those committed by another side, just as they are unable to pass moral judgement in academic terms. But what they can do when examining an event in history is to ask whether this is new, whether this is something hitherto unknown. Let me give you a simple example. Napoleon took almost as long to cross the Alps as Caesar had. The introduction of the railways however brought about an entirely new development. It was along these lines that I made my statement about the singularity of the murder of the European Jews. This is not a moral statement, it doesn't imply that other crimes should be condemned more or less severely. It is a purely rational, verifiable statement that this was something which had never occurred before in the history of mankind: that a particular group of people, defined as Jewish by a particular state when, after all, it is incorrect to categorize them as such, was to be exterminated by means provided by the state is without precedent. One has to think of cases like those which occurred in 1943 and 1944 when Germany had practically lost the war. Nonetheless the Jews in Oslo and Rhodes were rounded up and taken to the gas chambers in Auschwitz imposing a considerable strain on the bureaucracy.

I never used the word uniqueness, I always spoke about singularity, meaning something which had never occurred before. In connection with my statement about singularity I would like to cite another case. In 1943 a child was born in the Dutch transit camp of Westerbork. Because the infant was weak the Kommandant of the camp sent to Amsterdam for a bottle of brandy which he thought would help the child. It survived, but after a few weeks it was taken to Auschwitz. That is a small example of what I mean by singularity.

As to German-Soviet relations, Michael Stürmer spoke about the trauma of the Bolshevik Revolution of 1917 which affected the German and of course the English and French bourgeoisie, and Ernst Nolte has said that there probably is a casual nexus. One can spend a great deal of time speculating about this in rather general terms. But one can also state that Hitler did not perceive Bolshevism as a threat – he said as much on innumerable occasions – but as an opportunity. He said that this was advantageous to his cause because with the Revolution Jews had replaced the former German establishment in Russia, and since he did not think Jews were capable of leading a state, he saw Russia as a colossus with feet of clay, an expression he used time and again, and as an easy target for German expansionism. That, in short, was Hitler's philosophy and he stuck to it.

Incidentally, the only statesman Hitler always showed respect for was Joseph Stalin. Hitler despised Churchill because he thought

him incapable of identifying his own, that is to say, British interests.

A final observation. According to a conversation Goebbels
recorded in his diary in 1945, when all was lost, Hitler was
wondering yet again, if he could not manoeuvre himself out of
fighting a war on two fronts after all. He gave some thought to
the idea that he could perhaps negotiate with Stalin and not with
the Western powers.

RALF DAHRENDORF: The famine which Robert Conquest described
so dramatically in his book, *Harvest of Sorrow*, raises the question
of how it was technically possible to take away every scrap of
food from people who live off the land. One would think that
farmers would manage to tuck away the odd morsel to survive
at least.

ROBERT CONQUEST: There are various conceptual points, but
firstly I would like to stress again that I regard the Nazi crimes as
worse and that race theory is a more frightful thing than any
other ideological method. I was noting a few points of comparison
rather than parallels in the Kulak case and I quoted Grossman
not as evidence, although it is in part evidence since he is a
witness and when he writes about these matters in a novel it is
not therefore refuted as evidence. But I was quoting him for his
opinion on the matter. I think Samuel Ettinger will agree that
Grossman has a strong *locus standi* for making this comparison.

Jürgen Kocka asked about the numbers involved in the deportation of 1930–1 and said 300,000 were killed. Soviet sources
show that this figure is far too low. The Soviet press of the time
reveals that an absolute minimum of about five million people
were deported and it can be shown that not less than 17 per cent
died on the way. So that makes the figure a good deal higher
straightaway. Stalin told Churchill that dekulakization was a
matter of 'ten millions' and that most of them were 'wiped out'.
That was probably a rough figure. We are now being told in these
meetings in Moscow that the number of deportees, which I have
always held to be around ten million, was probably quite a bit
higher. They are talking about five million families. That would
raise the figure to a minimum of about 25 million, of whom a
third probably escaped leaving something like 16 or 15 million
deportees.

They were not deported to areas settled under the Tsars. It's true that Stolypin sent large numbers of settlers into Kazakhstan who didn't die. The Kulaks were sent to the far north, mostly to the Arctic (they were in their vast majority not, of course, 'Kulaks' even by Stalin's definition, but ordinary 'middle peasants' as Soviet writings now freely admit). Only about a third of them were sent to labour camps, the rest were given strips of land and left to live or die. Certainly not less than a third of them died, perhaps more.

If we take the figure of deportees to be only ten million that would mean that about 3.5 million perished. Almost all of the other third who were sent to labour camp died there: very few people who went to labour camp between 1935 and 1939 survived, not more than ten per cent at any rate. So the total death toll of the Kulak deportation can't be less than around seven million. Even when you get hold of Soviet figures such as Danilov's, it is impossible to tell exactly how to divide them between the Kulak deportations and the terror famine of 1932–3. Whichever way one looks at it, it seems that the figures are roughly the same, around seven million dead as a result of each.

Now to Dahrendorf's question about the famine. It was a conscious act, the areas of famine were blockaded, food was taken away from the people, nothing was brought in and they were not allowed to move. As to how it was done: in the first place collectivization had already meant that the peasantry was not in possession of the grain. This to my mind was, apart from ideology, the real reason for collectivization. The idea was to get the grain out of the control of the peasantry into state hands. Every grain of wheat went into the communal granary. Of course the peasants still had a little food, they hoarded it, they picked roots, they did all sorts of things. But the houses were searched regularly by groups called 'tow brigades' who went around with little rods, poking in every hole in the house or around the garden, seizing everything they found. By March 1933 every eatable leaf had been devoured and for about two or three months there was absolutely nothing to eat over a very large area including the Ukraine, the north Caucasus and the Don. Five million Ukrainians and about two million others died. That meant around 17 or 18 per cent of the Ukrainian population was wiped out, about a quarter of the rural population.

Stalin's method was not race theory, it was the method of the khans who would go through unruly territories harrying them with fire and sword. If one doesn't stick to modern history, there are plenty of parallels. It even happened in England in 1087. The method was to set fire to villages and kill a certain number of the population. Stalin used a slower method, starvation. But the principle is the same. He crushed the Ukraine in particular and at the same time he conducted a great campaign against the Ukrainian intellectuals, the head as it were of the nation, as the peasants were the body. Around 200 of the 240 odd writers of the Ukraine were shot or sent to camps at that time. And the Ukrainian Autocephalous Church was suppressed.

The question of cover-up was raised here and Jürgen Kocka asked to what extent opening up is going to strengthen or weaken the Soviet Union. There is an argument that if you keep things covered up, you keep the machine going, you keep the orthodoxy in existence. The progressive argument however is that absence of truth ruined the Soviet Union under Brezhnev. Unlike the Germans the progressives are not so much arguing about these events, they are too intent on getting the facts first or establishing their existence. My view, and I think it is not only shared by dissidents or the most progressive wing of the party, is that at least the appearance of having told the truth about the past will be a strength to the regime, if it can do it. It is in a delicate position, since some of the functionaries partly responsible for these actions are still around. It's not easy for the same party to say, I'm frightfully sorry, we killed millions of innocent people and we won't do it again. The regime has a moral albatross around its neck. It can perhaps be got rid of now, there are fewer people alive who were involved in the actual slaughters, but it is obvious why those brought up as members of the ruling caste don't want the subject raised. Others think revelations will weaken the image of the Soviet Union. As I mentioned, the Poles are asking about the Katyn massacre, for example. It has been said that once this question has been cleared up, Soviet-Polish relations will be strengthened. Well, yes, but at first there will be a great deal of ill-feeling when the truth is admitted. For a time it will be difficult and troublesome to be open. But I agree that in the long run, after a period of transition everybody will feel better if even half the truth, even the general truth is told. (If however all the files are destroyed the Soviets will to some extent have it both ways. They can tell the truth and yet it won't all be there.)

LORD DACRE: The question about the fear of communism as an element of the success of Nazism has come up several times. It seemed to me that there is a confusion between two dates. I entirely agree with Professor Jäckel and others that in the 1930s communism was not a threat, but we should really be looking at 1920–3. That is the time of the *Räterepublik* in Munich, the Italian elections of 1922, the attempted communist takeover in Silesia. That is the time when communism seemed a real threat and it was then that Nazism began. Of course the communist threat was used opportunistically. But I think it is arguable that one reason why the German establishment put itself behind Hitler, in spite of the anti-semitism which it did not share, was a fear of communism. In fact it stated that at the time.

JÜRGEN KOCKA: I would like to advocate that a clear distinction be made between the threat and the perceived threat of communism.

GORDON CRAIG: I'm a little worried about this and I tend to agree with Jürgen Kocka. But if one is going to talk about traumas induced by Bolshevism one might speculate whether the biggest trauma wasn't caused in the United States starting with the Red scare of 1919 and continuing to the present.

RALF DAHRENDORF: I have just come across an article in the *Neue Zürcher Zeitung* entitled 'Historikerstreit in der Sowjetunion'. It deals with a new piece by Afanasiev in which he bemoans the fact that for decades there has been an official truth and a private truth in the Soviet Union and that the two have very little to do with each other. For historians this was, as he put it, mental torture, a moral trauma. He demanded historical truth about everything and was attacked by a group of official historians. The article has provoked me to make the following comment: We have concentrated on comparing events. Perhaps it is equally important to compare the way in which people deal with events and the conditions historians are faced with in different countries.

But first of all, before we return to the German subject and discuss why these issues have become topical, let us turn further east and listen to what Carol Gluck has to say about Japan.

CAROL GLUCK: The title of my presentation is: 'The over-determined past', for reasons that I think will be obvious. Although I am a Japanese specialist, I have followed the debate of the German historians – occasionally astonished, sometimes aghast, but always mesmerized by it because of the similarities in the patterns of history-writing in Japan and Germany. The similarities are particularly important because Japan is obsessed with its singularity, with what the Japanese are apt to call their 'uniqueness'. By that they do not mean the moral uniqueness of any national horror like the Holocaust, but the opposite: the uniqueness of the Japanese character and of Japanese history.

Without ever having experienced the Fall of God, referred to in the earlier discussion about Germany, the Japanese burn with a seemingly perennial need for national identity. In history as well, Japanese exceptionalism – that is to say, Japan as the exception to the rules and the course of history – appears like a haze, a blight, and indeed often an end to conversation, as when one seeks an analysis and receives the reply, 'It is because it is so Japanese'. That is why the *Historikerstreit* is important to me and why I have spent some time trying to make it important to the Japanese. For however German it may seem, it is almost equally Japanese. That is what I wish to emphasize here. In order to do so, I must touch on the background of post-war Japanese historiography, for that is what is being revised. There is an original myth of Japanese renderings of the war, which came into being in the immediate post-war years. This 'Ur-mythos' was the product of a curious convergence of the Left – communists just released from prison, Marxists in the universities – and the Right – old liberals who have now become new conservatives – joined by the general population, General Douglas MacArthur, and Americans both in the occupation and in Washington. In 1945–6 this assorted spectrum of opinion shared the view that the war itself was a judgement on the past. Characterized as an unjust and catastrophic conflict, the war signalled to them Japan's disastrous swerve off the road to modernity, defined in Western terms. Modernization, it seemed, had progressed well enough from the late nineteenth century until it was undone by the militarism and expansionism of the 1930s.

The first post-war moral was thus an open judgement on the past, and it was simultaneously accompanied by a second, which made the war a charge to the future as well. In 1945 in the mood of liberation from war and what is called 'emperor-system fascism', the Japanese repeatedly invoked a new beginning. It was as if Japan willed itself an instant transformation from war to peace, from fascism to democracy, and this concentration on the present made the confrontation with the past essential to the policy of the future.

Thus there was not only a convergence of left and right but also a confluence of politics and history, which together formed the foundation of the new state. The consensus that emerged embodied two myths: the first was that of radical discontinuity. Japan had, and still has, a *Stunde null*, a point zero of such historic proportion that one can find it expressed in the enviably precise sentence: 'The present began at noon, August 15th, 1945', at the moment, that is, when the surrender was announced. No continuity was to be allowed from the pre-war period, other than dangerous survivals to be struggled against or thin threads of liberal pre-history, which might support the new post-war system.

This break in 1945 is rendered as absolute. It reminds one of Heredotus writing about gryphons and ants bigger than foxes. The new beginning is a myth, and it is paired with a second myth, that of modernity betrayed. Post-war Japanese historians developed a *Sonderweg* historiography, which echoes the German version almost verbatim, with the difference that the Japanese developed theirs immediately after the war and have clung to it since. Modern Japan was considered a failure not only because of the war, but also because of the lack of a bourgeois revolution in the nineteenth century, the flawed development of industrial capitalism without political democracy, and the survival of feudal elements from a traditional agrarian past. These elements together were responsible for a deviation from the appointed road of the modern West.

These two myths – radical discontinuity and modernity betrayed – formed a single narrative, which stated that the roots of the war lay at home in the economic, social and what the Japanese once called spiritual, but now call ideological, structures of the country. The villains were identified as the military, the bureaucracy, big business, the landlords, and the victims were identified as everyone else. This narrative was domestic in focus; there was little mention of international relations except as a consequence of these domestic factors. It was what Herbert Butterfield would have called a heroic narrative, a narrative whose figures are larger than life, with millions of victims clearly identified, and a manichean distinction between good and evil.

This heroic narrative appeared in several versions. The dominant historiography in Japan since 1945 has been Marxist. The Japanese Marxist tradition in the academy goes back to the late

1920s, and when Marxists were able to speak freely again after 1945, they resumed their critical view of Japan's modern history. Thus the orthodox view in Japan is a blend of Marxist and left-liberal, what the Germans would recognize as *links-liberal*. The Japanese call the two of them together the progressive view of history. The progressive historians adhere to a structural view of the causes of the war, the so-called 'root theory' of Japanese history, which holds that the origin of the war lay at the roots of Japanese society. The conservatives, who are the dominant political figures, offered a different version of the past. Prime Minister Yoshida, who was not unlike Adenauer in the role he played in post-war politics, tended to bracket the period. Such elision is sometimes labelled the 'stumble theory' of Japanese history, because it suggests that Japan was marching along quite briskly when it tripped on the way to modern times, and that trip and fall was the period of war from 1931 to 1945. The popular past, which offered another version of the same heroic narrative, subscribed to a simpler moral calculus. Here Pearl Harbor became one side of an equation, the other side of which was the atomic bombings of Hiroshima and Nagasaki. The balance of victimization achieved, the Japanese wholeheartedly committed themselves to the new 'Peace constitution' and to democracy.

All three versions of the history of the war – the progressive consensus, the conservative alternative, and the popular past – interacted with one another. What is important about the post-war heroic narrative that informed each of them is that it still survives today as something of an anachronism. Even now Japan calls itself 'post-war', despite repeated official pronouncements since 1955 that the post-war period has ended. The popular commemorations of the fortieth anniversary of the end of the war in 1985, for example, celebrated the current economic prosperity compared with the privation and hardship of the immediate post-war period, describing such glorious changes in daily life as the evolution of the washing machine from prehistoric to electronic forms. Essentially this was history viewed from the kitchen sink, based on the same narrative which emphasized the new beginning and the consequent peace and prosperity.

Meanwhile the Marxist and left-liberal historians have clung tenaciously for four decades to their own version. Every time it was threatened – and it was threatened with Japan's counterpart of neo-Nazism, a radical, nationalist right – the progressive intellectuals closed ranks to protect it. The narrative was threatened from the Right in the 1960s, when a revisionist view declared the Second World War to be the latest skirmish in Asia's hundred-year war of colonial liberation from the Western imperialist powers. It was threatened in the mid-1970s, when some critics allegedly 'revitalized' the post-war period by claiming that American occupation had been illegal in terms of international law. The progressive historians even closed ranks against respectable colleagues like the scholar who considered the chronology of twentieth-century Japan in terms of a period that ran from 1925 to 1955, thus bridging the unbridgeable date of 15 August 1945. He was loudly excoriated as a 'reactionary historian', than which one can be called no worse in the Japanese intellectual landscape.

In order to close ranks and keep the heroic narrative in place the progressive historians had to perform some extraordinary calisthenics, even chiropractic manipulations of the intellectual sinews, particularly in regard to the United States, which the post-war narrative had depicted first as the midwife of democracy until the Cold War, when it became the saboteur of that same democracy. Japanese progressives criticized the United States for having imposed democracy on Japan, not least because Americans wrote the new Japanese constitution. Democracy, they argued, had to grow from within and no real democracy could emerge from MacArthur's constitution. Yet now the progressives are defending the 'peace constitution' imposed by MacArthur against challenges from the Right, which wishes to revise it in the name of rearmament. People like Maruyama, who in many ways is the counterpart of Habermas, think it better to defend the peace constitution – and even the security treaty between Japan and the United States, against which the Left struggled for decades – than to get something worse. What seems worse is the threat to the political foundations of the post-war system. To the progressives the greatest nightmare is the return of pre-war patterns or postures.

Each time politics and history threaten to diverge in this way, historians and intellectuals rise to protect the polity against revisions of history. This worked rather well until the 1970s, when significant changes seemed to occur. The Japanese have two terms for their *Tendenzwende*. One is 'conservatization', and the other is 'the period of high growth', which is shorthand for changes that resulted from Japan's economic prosperity. The changes in the mid-seventies created a receptivity in the popular mind to public revisions of the recent past. Although this was not new, the revisions emerged in the eighties in a different environment, and this has given the Japanese *Historikerstreit*, which has gone on for thirty years, a different dimension.

First, the revisions of the eighties were not made by historians. They were initiated by politicians and intellectuals in the realm of public memory. Prime Minister Nakasone, who came to office in December 1982, declared that the time had come for the 'settling of accounts with the post-war period'. The resemblance to the German *Schlußstrich* is striking, if unwitting. Certainly the choice of words is unusual in Japanese, but the idea is resoundingly clear. In 1982 an attempt at textbook revision of Japan's aggression in China used the word 'advance' instead of 'invasion' – advance being the word used when one moves a chess figure. The Japanese Bitburg occurred in August 1985, when the prime minister decided to pay the first post-war official visit to Yasukuni, the shrine of the war dead, where not only the spirits of the common soldiers but also those of convicted war criminals are enshrined. He thought perhaps that the time had come when Japan no longer needed to apologize for its history. Like Kohl and his evocation of the 'grace of a late birth', Nakasone claimed to be able to say such things because he himself did not belong to the wartime generation. Political leaders have long visited the shrine as private citizens, but the fact that the prime minister chose to go in an official vehicle was significant enough to cause an uproar both inside and outside the country.

In 1986 a cabinet minister was dismissed for declaring that the Rape of Nanking was no worse than the atrocities committed by other powers. The Rape of Nanking is Japan's Holocaust, in that it stands for what is indeed the signal part of Japan's unmastered past: the war in China. Such public attempts at revision of the history of that war, coupled with proposals for flying the national flag and singing the national anthem in schools, and the establishment of a national history museum, suggested a new atmosphere of public remembrance.

But if the ideas themselves are not new, why is the revisionist seizure occurring now? It is of course obvious that, however prodigious the efforts of the older generation, it is not possible to transmit what the Japanese call 'personal war experience' to future generations. But the new generation is not yet the source of the revisions. Nor is revisionism occurring because of the anniversaries, since the Japanese have ritualistically celebrated the end of the war ever since the first anniversary in 1946. It is perhaps more a question of time. In the four post-war decades, Japanese economic success has made the search for a more respectable past more desirable. A resurgence of national pride and the perennial obsession with national identity, which have been mentioned here in connection with Germany, also apply with equal force to Japan.

A few points, however, have not been mentioned, and I think they may provide more important answers to the question: why revisionism now? First, the intellectual authority of the progressive consensus has waned, as has the authority of the conceptual framework of both the Marxist and left-liberals. This phenomenon is not confined to Japan alone. In a sense, what ended in the 1970s in terms of intellectual life was the nineteenth century. Those concepts which Japan had long since absorbed into its political bloodstream, whether liberal or Marxist, seemed no longer to apply. As a result there was a sense of intellectual crisis, of groping uncertainty, which persists. This is combined with the second unmentioned fact that political possibilities are being redefined. Ralf Dahrendorf mentioned Germany's not having a party of the right, but how do you suppose left and liberal Japanese intellectuals and historians feel, having had one party, the conservative party, in power since 1955. The other parties have grown weaker with time. Here the threat to the political status quo in a context where the alternatives are not clear, is a second reason for the current mood.

Third, and I think this is far more important for Japan than the other reasons, there is the change in international politics. The decline of the absolute power of the United States is not much mentioned in this dispute about history in Japan. Until recently Japan was able to keep a relatively low international profile within the framework of the alliance with the United States. This fact was reflected in the wholly domestic narrative about the causes of the war: Japan had made terrible mistakes in international relations, and it was not going to do so again. This statement may seem extreme, but it is a passable description of Japan's post-war foreign relations. In recent years the country has become increasingly uneasy, as it has been called upon to take international responsibility commensurate with its economic power. Japan has shied away from a visible global role. It has been glad to trade, though in order to do so it was largely dependent on the United States. Now the United States is acting tough again, invoking metaphors of war to describe the trading relationship.

Indeed several articles appeared on the occasion of the fortieth anniversary of the end of the war, stating that in the end it was Japan that won the war, and now it was war between the two countries again. The Japanese are extremely sensitive to this Japan-bashing and are now responding by bashing America in turn. Some of the anti-Americanism in Japan today – even the new media expression of anti-semitism, where the Jews are surrogates for the Americans – is due to Japan's current unease about its place in the world.

One possible alternative is to seek a place within the regional context, but that proves difficult for Japan, which is not a *Land der Mitte*. It is instead a country on the edge, and it is very edgy about being there. Japan is on the edge of Asia, but it thinks of itself as aligned with the West and has serious problems in dealing with its Asian neighbours. The fact that China, where Japan was at war from 1937 to 1945, takes second place in much of the history of what the Americans called (and the Japanese still follow them in calling) the Pacific War is historiographic evidence of this inability. Japan cannot deal with Asia, and the feeling of discomfort is mutual: The loudest outcry against the public revisions of history – against the visit to the shrine, the alteration in the textbooks, the education minister's remarks about the Rape of Nanking – came from Beijing, Seoul, Singapore and Taiwan, none of those people have forgotten the war and the depredations by Japan. Japanese revisions, which had originally moved in the direction of national pride, produced instead what is now called 'I'm sorry diplomacy', with the prime minister having to apologize to every Asian head of state for the most recent transgression in Japan's revision of the other country's history.

I would like to conclude by arguing rather strongly that in the Japanese case it is not history which is being revised. There are no new facts, there is no new material. What is being revised are the myths that have survived for so long, so anachronistically. Until 1945 is bridged, until the gryphons are confronted, the genesis of the post-war period cannot really be explained. It is impossible to explain where the post-war era came from if one refuses to connect it with the pre-war in any way other than by negation. Normal historical revision has ironically been made difficult by the well-intentioned efforts to keep so vigorous a collective memory alive for forty years. Myths, however, turn rather easily into their opposites, so that the current revision of myth is dangerous indeed. The consequences for Japanese domestic politics are considerable, but they are even more considerable for international relations. That applies most immediately to relations with Asia but also to those with the West.

What concerns me most about the *Historikerstreit* and about the Japanese revision of the period of the 1930s and 1940s, is the relentless strength of the categories of national history. Germany, Japan, the Soviet Union, and others – each of these countries was involved in a world war and yet in their histories of that war they have virtually left the world out. So, too, have the critics of revisionism. In other words, whether a champion of revisionism or a progressive critic, the categories remain wholly national. In Japan that means that this question lacks a properly international dimension. It seems to me that historians, at least, must rise to the challenge and confront history, without taking refuge in the comfortable categories of our respective national histories, and I include national identity as one of those comfortable categories. For we are talking about a late twentieth century world which will no longer permit such homely national histories of international events.

RALF DAHRENDORF: How do obvious continuities like the Emperor fit into this picture of the unbridgeable?

CAROL GLUCK: The Emperor is considered in the progressive consensus to be the single most objectionable and untenable institution that survived from the pre-war period. The progressives make major politics out of every issue related to the Emperor, including the fact that he was not tried as a war criminal. This has been going on for forty years and continues, most noticeably after Hirohito's death. The public, which is constantly being polled, says it does not care very much – decent, doddering old man and all that. The popular interest in the imperial institution is mild, Hirohito not having been a very charismatic figure. The Right used the Emperor in its allegations about the loss of national identity and national pride, which the abject view of the pre-war past has brought about. Hirohito was thus one of the most important symbols which each side used to advocate its version of the past.

WOLFGANG MOMMSEN: Carol Gluck has given a brilliant description of the destruction of those two founding myths and I found the reasons she gave for the current changes very convincing.

But I find it a little difficult to make out what is actually left. What form does the consensus which survives the myth take? Is it still modernity, is it a historical attitude, or is it a positive attempt to recapture the long-standing Japanese historical tradition? That would seem to contradict what Carol Gluck said.

CAROL GLUCK: I was struck by Lord Dacre's remarks because Japan has experienced an end of a similar kind to the one he mentioned that Germany witnessed in 1945. Something is breaking apart, certainly as far as the philosophy of history is concerned, and that is what I meant by the end of the nineteenth century. There is a loss of faith in the intellectual armamentarium of Japanese progressives, so what is left is somehow 'after modernity', and that is why Japan is currently so taken with the post-modern. The Japanese seek to identify something beyond the modern, but they cannot because the available conceptual frameworks fail them. The answer is that there is no new synthesis yet about the modern policy or about historical writing either.

As to the recapturing of the Japanese tradition and the revisions from the Right, the neo-nationalist revisions indeed talk a great deal about Japanese tradition, but despite what you read, these are still fringe groups in Japan, not the mainstream. Progressives fear that the figure of the Emperor will fill the vacuum left by the view of modernity that is no longer persuasive. As for Japanese tradition itself, the Japanese have assimilated so much of the West that it is no longer possible to separate Western tradition from the Japanese. They have a new Japanese tradition now, which has been reconstructed three times in the past 120 years, and it may be happening again. But the Japanese tradition is being reconstructed with what we would recognize as Western elements built into its very woodwork.

WOLFGANG MOMMSEN: I have always found it very striking that Japan is the greatest Max Weber consumer in the world. The Japanese seem to buy more books on or by Weber as well as producing many books which we unfortunately can't read. As far as I know, Weber seems to play an enormous role, in conjunction with Marx rather than against him, as a symbol of modernization. I don't know enough about Japan to understand why this should be so.

CAROL GLUCK: I think of it as the Marx-Weber industry of Japan, since it sometimes seems that the Japanese think of one person with a hyphenated name, Mr Marx-Weber. Wolfgang Mommsen is right, the two figures have coalesced, and this hyphenated thinker has provided a major source of social and political conceptualization. The interest in Marx-Weber began with the development of the academy and the structure of modern learning in Japan, which was taken over almost entirely from Germany. Japanese intellectuals and scholars of a certain age write a Japanese that is only intelligible if you know German, and even then you sometimes wonder at the German words rendered in Japanese characters.

This is partly explained by the history of the academy and partly by the intellectual context in Japan in the inter-war period, particularly in the 1920s, when there were two contending paradigms, both of which depended on the hyphenated thinker Marx-Weber. One was liberal – it is now referred to in Japan as modernist – and that was the Marx-Weber paradigm with the emphasis on Weber. The emphasis of the other one was Marx, and it proved stronger and, in the end, dominant. But these two paradigms together dominated Japanese intellectual life. The Japanese absorbed them and made their own theoretical contributions to the discourse. Weberian studies in Japan seem second only to Toyota in terms of being a national industry and I do not see any end to it, except that the authority is waning. The industry continues, the journals are published, but it does seem more mechanical now, as if in homage rather than living faith.

One can imagine how difficult it is to be a Marxist in Japan, which may well be the most bourgeois society in the world. The tenacity of the intellectual establishment has perhaps separated the Marxists from reality more than they would like. The intellectuals are aware of this, but they have nothing else to put in its place, and so there the progressive consensus stands, eroded but not replaced.

RALF DAHRENDORF: I'm not sure that I fully understood what Carol Gluck said about the quest for national identities being in a sense a sweet romantic notion in a world in which some of the basic constraints are international.

CAROL GLUCK: Certainly not a sweet romantic notion. The quest for national identity, which is endemic in Japanese life, should be declared out of the historian's court. Every time history has been used to create national identity in Japan, there has been a miscarriage, or at least that is how the Japanese see it. The progressives regard it as an abuse of history, which is associated with the years of ultra-nationalism and war, or with neo-nationalism in the present. Neither the case for history as providing national identity in Japan nor the case against it seems to be fruitful, if only because both sides repeat the same arguments and none of it leads to history-writing. It is more a manipulation of myths, which is not sweet and romantic but misbegotten, and we as scholars ought not to aid and abet it (even in criticism) by making such activity seem to be the proper task of historians.

JÜRGEN KOCKA: Has the historical profession resisted this redefinition of the general consensus in any way? We know that historical facts can be interpreted in different ways, but they cannot be interpreted in *any* way. There are limits to reinterpretation and there is a point at which one becomes a bad historian if one does not protest. I think we reached this point at certain stages in our *Historikerstreit*. Is there a tension within the historical profession in Japan created by these politically oriented attempts to re-define the consensus?

CAROL GLUCK: There is more than a tension. There is an outright battle. The historians, including even the so-called reactionary ones, have closed rank against this revision. They argue with it in what I call a mythical way, but they will not permit it to stand unchallenged. This is what I mean by the anachronism of the post-war consensus. It is such a strong canonical consensus that speaking about tension is putting it mildly. Japan could do with a Lord Weidenfeld, since I doubt that Japanese historians would ever gather in one room to debate their differences, so strongly do they hold them.

LORD WEIDENFELD: I have always wondered what it is in the tone or style of Japanese historians of the nineteenth or twentieth century that makes them incomprehensible and unpublishable in the West. Can anyone other than specialists like Carol Gluck mention a book by a contemporary Japanese historian which has made an impression, a first-rate work of historiography on the transition from medieval to modern Japan which has become a classic of world literature? Why is that?

CAROL GLUCK: It is a problem which also besets Japan in international relations and contributes to the country's obsession with its uniqueness. Perhaps it is a problem of cultural translation, of linguistic logic rather than of semantics. Japanese works cannot be literally translated into English, they have to be rewritten. This is a formidable job because the person who rewrites the text has to know almost as much as the original author. I am loath to say this because I do not want to aid the cause of Japanese exceptionalism in any way, but it is a particularly Japanese problem. We are trying to surmount it with some fairly hefty rewritings, which only some scholars will stand for, as you may imagine.

LORD DACRE: It seems to be a difficulty that only works one way because every book written in English can be translated into Japanese.

CAROL GLUCK: Every language can be – and is – translated into Japanese.

LORD WEIDENFELD: And it does not apply to fiction, it applies to non-fiction books, to biographies and memoirs.

CAROL GLUCK: This has to do with the logic of expository prose. The reason it does not apply the other way round is that the Japanese have two languages: they read Japanese and they read a Japanese which is 'translatese', which they have learned the way we might learn Dutch. Westerners, on the other hand, have no experience and little inclination when it comes to learning 'Japlish'.

LORD ANNAN: Is the difference between the German experience and the Japanese possibly this, that in Germany the Nazi period produces a sense of profound guilt about the actions of the past, whereas Japan, being in Riesman's terms a more tradition-directed society, feels not guilt but shame about its past? What do you do with shame? Read any of the Greek dramatists. Read the novels of Shusaku Endo or Kazuo Ishiguro. Rather than admit that you performed a shameful act you say, some God did this, some God jogged my arm and I killed him, you invent reasons for exculpating yourself. The best way to deal with shame is to sweep the thing under the carpet as quickly as possible. Then you can work, then you can live again. Whereas guilt is a burden which one can only get rid of by talking and talking and talking about it.

CAROL GLUCK: In a word, no. First of all the Asians do not use the word guilt. The word used in connection with the war is responsibility. The Japanese have spent the last forty years publicly flagellating themselves about the fact that there was no resistance, that there was no exile, internal or external, that the Japanese people submitted to the excesses of their government. They have publicly and aggressively maintained this memory, in some ways they have maintained it more aggressively, more continuously than the Germans because the heroic narrative remained so strong in Japan. It has not been historicized in the sense that a tidily mastered past is also a past made historical.

MICHAEL STÜRMER: I have sometimes had the feeling that the Japanese whom I have met felt more shame about losing the war than about their performance during the war. But on a more serious note, do you think that one of the many differences between Japan and the European countries is the absence of the Christian notion of guilt, sin and conscience? Perhaps I should not say absence, but doesn't the totally different character of these notions, if they exist, explain a great deal about the present moral situation?

CAROL GLUCK: No, but it would take me days to explain why this is not so. I can only entreat you not to introduce these concepts as a way of explaining the difference. Take my word for it, the lack of a Christian tradition is not the pivotal difference. There is plenty of guilt and there is plenty of conscience. Ruth Benedict's analysis of guilt-shame is true in a certain context, but I would not use those explanations in the context of the war and national memory.

In view of the lack of time, Ralf Dahrendorf suggested the conference close the discussion about Japan for the time being and asked Michael Stürmer to deliver his paper.

MICHAEL STÜRMER: The historians' debate is, as we have all learned, a double misnomer. It is not academic, nor is it a debate. Gordon Craig has called it 'the war of the German historians'. Sadly, some of the rules of fair play which constitute academic debate have gone overboard. Even the fundamental rule that historians must check their sources was sacrificed on the altar of enlightenment in accordance with the old maxim: let the end justify the means. In fact, since 1983 it has not become uncommon to cultivate moral assassination by implying that other historians secretly sympathize with the Nazi past. This is still going on. The irony is that Jürgen Habermas, well known as the prophet of *herrschaftsfreier Diskurs*, discussion without repression, has engaged in this very game.

I would like to offer three tentative answers to this question, why such a debate now? I think there were other occasions when this debate might have begun, but did not. Let me cite two examples. One occasion was the publication by the magazine *Stern* of the supposed Hitler diaries, when it was claimed that they presented a completely new *Führer* and that Nazi history would more or less have to be rewritten: a mild, ignorant *Führer* floating above the clouds with his henchmen doing the dirty work. If the diaries had been genuine, it would indeed have been necessary to revise our view of Hitler's role. Real evidence should certainly never be withheld. The point is, however, that the editors of *Stern* seem to have been so taken by this new view of Hitler that they printed the diaries (plus commentary pointing to the necessity of re-assessing his role) without making sure that the documents were what they purported to be. At least a moment of thought should have been given to that. There are others in this room who know the inside story. I will restrict myself to quoting one of my venerable colleagues at this table who said in 1984, referring to that bizarre and bitter incident (and I quote from the legal proceedings): 'Dazu sagt mir meine Errinnerung nichts' ('my memory fails me').

The second example is the controversy surrounding Fassbinder's abominable play *Der Müll, die Stadt und der Tod*. It is about a post-Nazi Jewish property speculator in Frankfurt. The play was not performed during Fassbinder's lifetime but the author stipulated that the premier had to be in Frankfurt before it could be put on any other stage. When the Frankfurt theatre made moves to stage the anti-semitic play it was not the intellectuals who argued against it; rather it was the newspapers, it was the

Frankfurter Allgemeine Zeitung that shot it down. This pathetic play received the final *coup de grâce* at the hands of Joachim Fest and I don't think he has been given enough credit from those quarters which, I feel, should also have joined his battle. The *Stern* affair died because of its inherent stupidity and the Fassbinder affair was killed by the *Frankfurter Allgemeine*.

I cannot provide an answer to the question why the debate took place when it did, but I have observed four coincidences. The first coincidence is that the debate coincided with the federal election campaign at the end of January 1987. The second coincidence is that some of the political parties involved in the election were conspicuously lacking, not short-term operative arguments, but a sense of direction. Peter Glotz, then secretary-general of the SPD, was not the only one to say that the Left had lost intellectual and cultural hegemony.

The third coincidence was that on 2 July 1986 a hearing was held by the SPD, the major opposition party in Bonn about government plans for the future German Historical Museum in Berlin. It turned out to be a little difficult to condemn this project outright. To begin with, the party was divided. People like Richard Löwenthal did not think it a bad idea. Others thought it would have been a very good idea if the old plans of Willy Brandt or Richard von Weizsäcker or Heinemann, in which Eberhard Jäckel was also involved, had been realized, perhaps in a slightly modified way. The advisory committee set up by the CDU government had sixteen members, among them eminent people like Jürgen Kocka and Richard Löwenthal whose SPD affiliation is well-known, two colleagues for whom I have a great deal of respect, not least after having worked with them on that committee. The committee was intent on achieving a consensus, and it succeeded. I was therefore somewhat surprised when I heard that Jürgen Habermas – not known for his museum expertise or as a historian – was invited to give the keynote address at the SPD hearing. In this speech he attacked four historians, the 'gang of four'. Three of them had literally nothing to do with the plans for the Berlin museum. The fourth one, the publisher Wolf Jobst Siedler, had not written anything offensive, nor had he done much work on the Nazi period. Furthermore, Habermas presented Siedler as the mastermind behind that sinister revisionist conspiracy. As it happens, Siedler had been sentenced to death by the Nazis for helping Jews in hiding, not exactly the kind of man one would depict as the head of such a sinister operation.

The forth coincidence: Habermas' great 'J'accuse' appeared in
Die Zeit where the passages referring to Siedler were omitted. *Die
Zeit* however forgot to mention that the author had presented his
arguments the week before at the SPD hearing.

If one disregards the muddle-headedness of the debate, which
was due to the fact that six or seven arguments were going on at
the same time on different levels, I think one could say that there
are three groups or arguments. Two of these are visible and one
is not, one group is historical, another political and a third is what
I, in shorthand, would call Freudian. I am not going to comment
on the Freudian aspect.

Given the present German situation, the political, moral and
economic environment, historians would be well advised to
engage in a number of debates – again, debates which never
happened. For instance on technology and the lost notion of
progress, or on nuclear weapons and the psychology of the mass
society in Germany and, for the sake of comparison, elsewhere.
One could have debated the situation of a divided Germany in a
changing world and the question of how the two German societies
which are so different and yet share so many assumptions relate
to one another. Perhaps we spent too much time on the one issue
so that there wasn't time to engage in other debates, but it is not
too late to do so in the future.

As to the second group of assumptions, I think that the underlying reasons for what some call a 'debate' and others would
call 'the war of the German historians', or an attempt at moral
assassination, lie deeper and do indeed deserve our attention.
The ramifications and the unspoken assumption of the post-war
settlement are changing rapidly and with potentially dramatic
results, be they beneficial or not so beneficial. I am thinking of
the concept of the 'Pax Americana', the Western assessment of the
Soviet threat or the simple fact that many historical assumptions
which were taken for granted in the immediate post-war era need
explanation now, because in biblical terms forty years are enough
to change the unspoken assumptions of a people. The Jews had
to wander in the desert for forty years before they were admitted
to the promised land. The basic rationale behind this was that a
nation or a group undergoes considerable changes in the course
of forty years.

First and foremost, one must not forget that Germany is a
divided country. Both parts of this country were stigmatized and
traumatized for a long time and in some ways still are. Two factors

cannot be ignored: people search for moral reassurance in their personal or collective past, and the partition of the country into two conflicting philosophical and political systems tended to create a special dynamism. The East German feeling of *nous, les autres, noi altri* or, in German, *wir, die anderen* is gradually being replaced by what Wolfgang Seiffert from Kiel, a former East German, now West German economist and a one-time advisor to Honecker, calls the 'cultural Piedmont role' of the GDR. He may be wrong, he may be right. At any rate he knows what he is talking about.

I would have liked more comment from some of my colleagues when the GDR put back the statue of Frederick – as Honecker said – 'the Great' back in its original place on Under den Linden, and perhaps a little more comment on interesting exhibitions like the 'Splendour of Dresden'; a little more comment, too, on why the reconstruction of East Berlin is being undertaken in the way it is. My local paper in Erlangen denouncing all those who care about a German historical museum in West Berlin, is delighted by the Germanness of East Germany and wants the West Germans to go to East Germany to find their roots. I don't take that too seriously, but nowadays you come across dozens and dozens of such statements, not only on the Left. Of course, Germany does not end on the Elbe-Werra line. But is there not an ambiguity? Should we not begin to worry about this ambiguity and make a conscious effort to overcome it? This is not to argue for counter-ideologies, which are always futile. But we should take a longer view.

Another fundamental change has taken place since 1986 – Christian Meier has already referred to it. It has to do with the breakdown of 'progressism', or the belief in progress. After 1945, especially at the time of the 'economic miracle' and under the chancellorship of Willy Brandt, progress seemed to triumph. The government was seen purely as the administrator of progress and of increasing welfare. But in 1972, the year before the oil crisis, the Club of Rome published *The limits to growth*. Then the oil-crisis struck. In the mid-1970s the fear of nuclear deterrence took on a serious dimension, and the fear of nuclear energy climaxed with Chernobyl. Now even the promise of unlimited promiscuity has fallen on hard times due to AIDS. The notion of progress has collapsed, alas, and this has changed the political spectrum. If no one believes in progress any more, where does that leave the conservatives? There is a strange reversal of values with Left wing

SPD figures like Eppler or Lafontaine presenting themselves as the real conservatives, whereas the CDU is left with technological enthusiasm and economic growth. This is not a good thing, because it is unnatural. *Tendenzwende* is not a new expression. It was coined in 1974 after the oil shock and found its expression in Helmut Schmidt, long before Helmut Kohl took office.

The third assumption is that the Federal Republic of Germany has to redefine its place in time and space. Changes at home and in the world at large are too momentous for Germans to be able to continue as if nothing had happened. It is difficult to go on writing the history of progress if society as a whole has lost faith in progress. In his memoirs Henry Kissinger described the Federal Republic of Germany as an economy in search of political purpose. He compared it to a tall tree with shallow roots which can be felled overnight by a sudden spring storm. Whether we believe this to be so or not, the picture painted by the international wizard is not reassuring for the Germans or for their neighbours. A great deal has happened to underline this view since Kissinger published his memoirs in 1976.

Ralf Dahrendorf called on Eberhard Jäckel to read his paper.

EBERHARD JÄCKEL: Although I was tempted to intervene in the debate earlier on, I did not do so because Ralf Dahrendorf had asked me to prepare a paper on precisely the questions which have been discussed until now, that is, what the *Historikerstreit* was about and way it broke out at this particular time. Any past, be it individual or collective, is difficult to live with and a difficult past is particularly difficult to live with. It can be accepted or repressed, it can be rejected and denied, it can be justified and condemned, glorified or demonized, it can be used for political or other purposes. But however you wish to define it, it is a touchstone for political culture.

There can be no doubt that the Nazi past is a particularly difficult one. The German reaction to it has, however, been remarkably constant. There are only a few patterns and they keep recurring with minor modifications. Denial was impossible from the beginning. Stalin could deny Trotsky but the Germans could never deny Hitler. In a free society the past cannot be denied. In West Germany research has been free, the archives are accessible, historians were never hampered and they produced honourable results. Outright justification was equally impossible. It was prevented by the Nazis themselves, their crimes were too obvious.

So the Nazi past could only be accepted or repressed. The question however was: what relative place should it be given in public life? Repression or reducing the role to the Nazi period in public life became increasingly difficult. The debate about the past therefore took different forms. In the 1950s there was first of all the appeal to draw the line, *einen Schlußstrich ziehen*. Democracy had been re-established, de-nazification formally completed, the book could be closed. This never meant denial, it meant that there should be no more incrimination and less public debate about the Nazi past. The parliaments of several *Länder* decided to close the archives on de-nazification and there are *Länder* where they are closed by law even today. In at least one case it was proposed that these archives should not only be closed but destroyed. It was like putting the past on a ship and making it sink. But it proved to be unsinkable.

The formula for drawing the line was discredited and is no longer in use. It had been supported by a historical theory which enjoyed a great deal of popularity among scholars in the 1950s and was eagerly accepted by public opinion with far-reaching political consequences. This was the theory of totalitarianism, *die Totalitarismusthese*. In simple terms it stated that this century had seen two kinds of totalitarianism, Bolshevism on the one hand, and Fascism or Nazism on the other. Nazism was seen as a defensive reaction to Bolshevism, that is to say, whatever its shortcomings or excesses, Nazism had at least been anti-Bolshevist. In accordance with this theory the war against the Soviet Union was widely regarded by historians and the public as a preemptive war. Certain groups have stuck to this view. While the theory of totalitarianism amounted to a partial justification of the Nazis, its political implications were far more important. This was the time of the Cold War and the Federal Republic had been established as a stronghold against communism. While anti-communism enabled Germans to regain sovereignty in conducting their foreign affairs, domestically anti-communism became the bridge over which the former Nazis could enter democracy. Here, at least, was continuity. It permitted reconciliation and integration on the one hand, it became the real cement of the Federal Republic. This could be called the anti-totalitarian consensus. It prevented neo-Nazism on a serious scale, because Nazis could be integrated over that bridge, and at the same time it prevented full acceptance of the Nazi past, as the necessary condition of integration was drawing the line.

The Nazi past did not pass away. On the contrary, in the late 1960s and '70s it drew nearer and nearer. In time more and more Nazi crimes came to light. What is called the Holocaust became ever more visible. Sensibility increased. The young generation of 1968, Hitler's children as they have been called, renounced the consensus provided by the theory of totalitarianism. At the same time Willy Brandt's *Ostpolitik* rendered the old anti-communist pattern partially obsolete. The German right desperately opposed *Ostpolitik* and the integration came to an end. Then came the change of government in Bonn in 1982. It was expected by some to be more than just a change of cabinet, it was to be *the* change, *die Wende*, a return to the old consensus.

I think the turning point came in May 1985 when two events revealed two different reactions to the Nazi past, all the more painfully as they involved the ruling party. On the one hand there was the president, Richard von Weiszäcker, who accepted the Nazi past in his famous address of 8 May. In the same week there was, on the other hand, the Bitburg incident. This can be seen as an attempt to repress the past, since the meaning of Chancellor Kohl's gesture – which was incidentally in such marked contrast to Willy Brandt's gesture when he fell to his knees in Warsaw – of course was to draw the line once more, this time by reconciliation over the graves. But reconciliation with the United States had been achieved long ago and, absurdly enough, it was being compromised now for the first time. However, it became apparent that what lay behind the visit to Bitburg was a different reaction to the past, all the more so since the suggestion to go to a concentration camp on the occasion had originally been refused.

In my opinion this was the origin of the *Historikerstreit*. The dispute cannot be understood without Bitburg. When Herr Nolte and Herr Fest began talking about singularity this was nothing but a new attempt at de-singularizing and normalizing the Nazi past. Their assertion that Auschwitz was a pre-emptive reaction to the gulag was nothing but a reprise of the old theory of totalitarianism. Since these arguments were not taken up in the debate – neither Herr Nolte nor Herr Fest replied to my counter arguments – it soon became apparent that the so-called historians' dispute had nothing to do with historical controversy. It was a political debate about two different reactions to the past, about values, about the evaluation of the Nazi past. Habermas' violent and, historically, largely incompetent reaction was only comprehensible when seen against the background of Bitburg. He had incidentally written an article on Bitburg in 1985 and that may be called the beginning of the *Historikerstreit*. Initially outside observers may have found the controversy confusing, at least I did, but then the conflicting positions became crystal clear. What may be called the conservative position is that the Nazi past is a burden and its relative place in public life should be reduced. When Herr Stürmer deplored the loss of the anti-totalitarian consensus, he appealed for a return to the theory of totalitarianism and when he characterized the German condition with the phrase *viel jüngste Geschichte und wenig aufrechter Gang*, much recent history and little self-assurance, he meant it – and I hope to be fair and present this as objectively as I can – very seriously. I regard it as a very serious proposition that in order to be self-confident Germans must talk less about recent history. That is exactly what Herr Dregger, the chief whip of the CDU–CSU, meant when he said a little earlier that *Mißbrauch der Vergangenheitsbewältigung*, abusing coming to terms with the past, could render the Germans *zukunftsunfähig*, incapable for the future. And it is what Herr Strauß meant when he said that the Germans must at last step out of the shadow of the Third Reich. When Kohl compared Gorbachev to Goebbels and asserted that there were concentration camps in the GDR, the anti-totalitarian frame of reference was evident. I could cite more examples, but instead I want to press on to describe what may be defined as the liberal position.

The liberals maintain that the Nazi past should be fully discussed and accepted because it is the only honourable way to deal with it. They also believe that, although it is a burden, the Nazi past can, at the same time, be an asset because it increases sensibility to the values of freedom, peace, democracy and human rights, that the Nazi past can be regarded as a strength rather than as a burden that needs lightening. The so-called *Historikerstreit* has come to an end, but the underlying struggle between the two positions seems to be continuing in different fields. I don't have time to quote as many examples as I would wish, but here is one. When Norbert Blüm, the German minister of employment, recently protested against torture in Chile, and Pinochet remarked that a German had no right to do so, Blüm retorted that it was precisely the Nazi past which not only entitled him to fight for human rights, but obliged him to do so. Blüm said, 'das ist meine Form der Wiedergutmachung' – that is my way of making amends. The opposite stance was expressed by Franz Josef Strauß, when he claimed that the Chilean putsch in 1973 had at least been a mighty blow against international communism.

Those who adhere to the conservative position are fighting an uphill battle, and that worries me. Internationally and to a great extent nationally as well, Nolte and Fest were almost totally isolated. *Ostpolitik* is an established fact. The German Right lost ground in the federal election of January 1987. Kohl, who had wanted to visit Bitburg only, was finally forced by public opinion to go to Bergen-Belsen as well. The fierce conservative opposition to Gorbachev's disarmament proposals had to be given up. Losing fighters tend to become desperate. I fear, therefore, that we will probably see more and worse outbursts of that antiquated conservatism which has already done so much damage to Germany's international standing. The reaction to the Nazi past is a perfect touchstone. It enables one to pass judgement on the political culture in a given country, in this case on Germany's political culture.

JOACHIM FEST: To be frank, I scarcely recognized myself in the caricature which Eberhard Jäckel has drawn. He obviously rates me among what he calls the conservative wing of the Federal Republic, and by that he means those groups who believe that the Germans should spend less time reflecting on their past, less time looking back on the recent past, that they should at last step out of the shadow of the Hitler period.

EBERHARD JÄCKEL: I didn't say that.

JOACHIM FEST: Well, Herr Jäckel, speak less about it then, and 'normalize' the past, Auschwitz in particular, that was one of the expressions you used. I don't want to repeat what I have already said about my work in the past years: it amounts to quite the opposite. Indeed I entirely agree with Herr Jäckel that it is possible to draw strength from the burden of the past. But enough of that.

Herr Jäckel said that the theory about the line finally being drawn was first propagated in the 1950s. As far as I can remember, I may be wrong, things were very different. Academics and journalists only began working off the Nazi period in the fifties. Until then the Germans had hardly examined or analyzed anything. Most of the publications on the Third Reich had been

written by English and American historians. Under these circumstances, how could it have been possible to seriously advocate
'drawing the line'? A few politicians may have advocated this,
indeed, some did, but, as the following years show, they were
disregarded without further ado.

Herr Jäckel then went on to say that the theory of totalitarianism aroused renewed interest in the discussion of the Third
Reich because this theory had, he said, more or less reconciled
the Germans with their past, that it led the way to exoneration.
According to Jäckel's interpretation of the theory, the Nazi regime
had opposed Bolshevism, it had stood against one form of totalitarianism and that stance had, after all, more or less justified it.
In this way it had become acceptable to the German conscience.
This interpretation is distorted. Herr Jäckel knows as well as
anyone else that the theory of totalitarianism was developed by
Hannah Arendt and others in the forties. Hannah Arendt was
certainly the last person who would have wished to justify
National Socialism or, although she could hardly have predicted
that tendency at the time, to play the means for reconciliation
with the past into the hands of those Germans who were wanting
to suppress what had happened.

Speaking of this I would like to recall a conversation I had with
Hannah Arendt in the late sixties, since it has a direct bearing on
the core of our dispute. Asked about the impulse which led her
to write the book which became one of the fundamental texts on
the theory of totalitarianism she answered: The Jews are often
accused of thinking only of their own victims, of the persecution
and the pogroms they went through, that the Holocaust (which
of course was not referred to by that term at the time), had pushed
everything else aside. This book, she said, was also to be a sort of
commemorative monument, she used the word 'Erinnerungsmal',
to the victims who belonged to other groups or nations. I was
very impressed by these remarks.

But, to get back to the initial question: Herr Jäckel would surely
not want to accuse Karl Dietrich Bracher for example – who is
probably the most committed advocate of the theory of totalitarianism today – of having adopted this theory in order to
promote some exonerative or apologetic needs, or to help suppress
the past. I find all that fairly absurd, I can't think of another word
to describe it.

Then Jäckel spoke of Bitburg as the origin of the historians'
dispute, and here too he puts me in the camp of those who want

to shirk the burden of the past. I have commented on Bitburg on several occasions, and have said that it was a foolish act. I see no reason to change this view. Bitburg was unnecessary, pointless and even damaging to German interests. But unlike Herr Jäckel, who seems to see nationalistic rancour in everything, I think the government stumbled into this rather clumsily. If I remember correctly, Bitburg was originally chosen because it was, and still is, regarded as an example of a place where French, Germans and Americans are living in concord, something which is by no means a matter of course after generations of hatred and resentment. Officials decided on Bitburg after inspecting it in winter when snow covered the graves. Not until spring did they discover, somewhat to their dismay, that some members of the SS lay buried there. This is how scandals sometimes occur – due to coincidence and carelessness. But I don't share the view that this was the prelude to a calculated signal for a nationalistic turn of events as Herr Jäckel evidently suspects. At any rate, if it was a signal, I failed to recognize it.

A final remark which complements what I have already said about publishing Nolte's piece. In an old-fashioned way I stand, as I am learning here, a little more on the side of enlightenment than many of those who have grabbed the concept of enlightenment for themselves. I therefore believe that the issues which are the subject of the dispute can, and should, be solved academically but not politically. At this point I would like to mention something I discussed with Saul Friedlander earlier on. He asked me why I opposed the performance of the Fassbinder play, whereas I had taken a different stance in this dispute. The answer is simple: the performance of the Fassbinder play is a question of tact, of consideration, also of moral taste, and it must be said that the Germans have neither the right nor any reason to disregard the feelings which had been so deliberately hurt by the play. The Jews in the Federal Republic and everywhere else in the world should be spared this coarse, stereotypical portrayal of a Jew, who, to top it all, is not even given a name. He is simply presented as a stereotype.

This dispute is different. It is about issues which have nothing to do with taste or consideration. It is about truth or error, about questions which should and need to be thought about. Not to recognize this, to stifle the discussion with oral disqualifications and social and academic boycotts, as has been and still is the case, is, I think, questionable, to put it mildly. Perhaps it is another form of suppression. The constant search for the motives behind certain views, which we have been able to observe here again, should be mentioned in this context. It is as though one only ever put forth a new idea with a secondary motive or in pursuit of some political strategy: to rehabilitate the Nazi period, to reconcile the Germans with their history, to reduce the blame or the responsibility, to exonerate or to dispose of the past. It is apparently impossible or at any rate abstruse for anyone to want to express in a debate what he believes to be right. All this reveals an increasing tendency to ideologize and politicize historical science. It is a worrying practice because it destroys the prerequisites for discussion.

Eberhard Jäckel wanted to reply to this, but in view of the lack of time Ralf Dahrendorf suggested that others should be allowed to speak instead, as he wanted to avoid the discussion turning into a dispute between Fest and Jäckel.

JULIUS SCHOEPS: Before making a few remarks I would like to emphasize again that I speak as a Jew and as a citizen of the Federal Republic. I see certain developments rather differently from the way in which they have been depicted here. I would like to address four issues: Firstly, what I call the political culture of disorientations; secondly, the 'enlightenment' after 1945; thirdly, the populistic anti-semitic syndrome; and fourthly, the attempts to create a positive German identity.

We have already heard that for the first two post-war decades silence reigned about what happened in Germany after 1933. The schools I went to did not teach anything on that subject. We were taught history up to World War One; history 'stopped' after that event. Many people of my generation will confirm this fact, it should be borne in mind because it illustrates the situation. I think the educational system in the Federal Republic has failed in this respect. The reasons for this failure are multifold but the West German universities have something to answer for. After 1945 they did not try to reinstate those academics who had been driven away or were thrown out of Germany. Only a few attempts were made here and there to bring back former colleagues. No official statement was ever made on behalf of a chancellor or a president inviting those who had been expatriated to return.

So where did this 'enlightenment' take place? It is my conviction that it took place in the media and that it was the work of committed journalists, who had begun to examine the past at an early stage. They accomplished a great deal. I appreciate Joachim Fest's contribution in this context. But the fact remains that the universities did very little, and they only started to make a move in the right direction in the late seventies.

Yet, in my view, the populistic anti-semitic syndrome in West Germany is far more important. 1945 is not a watershed in German history; it is no zero hour. Certain recurrent patterns of behaviour, structures, feelings, prejudices persist and are passed on to the next generation. A study conducted in 1975 by Alphons Silberman, the Cologne sociologist, showed that fifteen per cent of the West German population were openly anti-semitic whilst thirty per cent were latently anti-semitic. These figures correspond with similar investigations in Austria. The significant statistic is the thirty per cent of latent anti-semites. As a result, anti-semitism surfaces under certain circumstances. The Waldheim affair in Austria illustrates this phenomenon; and there are similar cases in the Federal Republic. I agree with Eberhard Jäckel that questions raised by Bitburg, by the Fassbinder controversy, and the *Historikerstreit*, all are part of the same problem and that is what I call the eruption of the populistic anti-semitic syndrome. This and not Nolte's article and the discussions about the singularity of the Holocaust is at issue. Of course, Ernst Nolte is entitled to ask his question, but it is scandalous that established historians in post-World War II Germany suggest that Jews declared war on Hitler and that Tucholsky wanted Germans killed in gas chambers. It is outrageous that hardly anybody attacked Nolte for making such assertions. Instead everybody addressed the question of singularity regarding the Holocaust. Nobody seemed to have taken notice of the growing populistic anti-semitism in West Germany.

I would like to draw attention to a study of instances of vandalism in Jewish cemeteries in the Federal Republic since 1945. The statistics drawn from police records reveal 800 acts of vandalism in that period. But the actual number of cases is estimated to be much higher. The study shows that the frequency of such attacks has been increasing since the late seventies. We think it has something to do with the television film *Holocaust* which was broadcast in West Germany in 1978. It set something in motion. In the week following the broadcast there was a steep increase in vandalism of Jewish cemeteries; nearly twenty such acts were registered. Characteristically, the results of this research have not been accepted by officials in the Federal Republic. It is extremely important that this matter be given careful consideration and support, in order to avoid the suppression of which we are constantly speaking.

The attempt to create a German positive identity has curious repercussions, one of which is the argument regarding memorials commemorating the victims of National Socialism. I do not want to discuss who should be actually classified as a victim. I would like to draw attention to the fact that over the past two or three years, memorials have been set up in every little West German town and village; synagogues such as the one in Celle are being restored. A Gestapo cellar in Düsseldorf has been turned into a memorial as well, and high school students are brought to see it to keep the memory of the past alive. In my opinion such endeavours have the opposite effect. I do not think that young people like to be forced by badly trained teachers to adopt a penitential pose. We have never seen the consequences of such instructions. Those who study the intellectual subculture in the Federal Republic will find strange and alarming developments, for example, the magazine *Wir Selbst*, ('We Ourselves') which is subtitled *National Identität und internationale Solidarität*, (National Identity and International Solidarity). This publication has been in existence for a few years and has become increasingly popular even in intellectual circles. The ideas propagated by this journal go back to the theories of the national revolutionaries in the Weimar Republic. The existence and popularity of such a journal signals the rise of extremely dangerous tendencies whose consequences cannot be foreseen. I think we should watch this development. Michael Stürmer has said that a nation must be predictable. I agree.

HAGEN SCHULZE: So far we have been told about what is happening in the Federal Republic largely in terms of, the technical word is, a neo-conservative turn of the tide, also of a mood which has spread not only in intellectual and political circles, but among wide sections of the population. This tendency gives cause for renewed concern. But I am not sure that this is an accurate description of what is going on. Something is happening, but I have the feeling that we are faced with a different problem. Politicians are inclined to justify their deeds by referring to history. That is normal. Historians are constantly being called upon by politicians to help them with this. They frequently and willingly oblige, indeed, their delight in the power which they enjoy secondhand, so to speak, is often evident. Every academic has to decide for himself to what extent he should become involved in politics and to what extent he should keep his distance. This is not a new issue, it has been going on in Germany, particularly in connection with the matters we have been discussing, ever since the sixties, except that a different group of historians has been called on since the late sixties, early seventies. But the purpose has not changed.

When talking about setting up a German historical museum it is all too readily forgotten that in the early seventies we did actually create a historical museum. This museum was founded with obvious intentions of *Sinnstiftung*, endowment with meaning; the content was clearly manipulative and presented a distorted picture. I am speaking of the 'Gedenkstätte für die deutschen Freiheitsbewegungen', the memorial to the German struggle for freedom, in Rastatt. Ostensibly, the purpose was to legitimize the constitutional basis of the Federal Republic by drawing on events in German history with traditions of liberty, resistance and liberalism: the image begins with the medieval peasants' revolt, which probably never took place, continues through the peasants' rebellions in early modern times, the enlightenment, the history of the labour movement, the resistance during the Third Reich and so on. The Third Reich as such, national socialism, especially the Holocaust, are not touched on. They did not occur! I cannot remember a single article by a German historian criticizing this omission.

At about the same time a historical museum was set up in Frankfurt. There the history of the twentieth century was depicted in terms of the excesses of capitalism and liberalism culminating in fascism. The Holocaust was not featured while the subjugation of German workers was dealt with in depth. Since the Holocaust did not fit into the concept, only one picture was wedged in amongst many others with almost no explanation, and that was it. Now another museum is being created, and this time there is a public outcry, the historians are shrieking and there is a lively debate.

I would like to know what is going on among historians and intellectuals who previously did not dream of being critical of the use of German history for political purposes, and who did not criticize the fact that the Holocaust and the extermination of the Jews were dealt with in a totally inadequate way, if at all. But now they are pounding on Ernst Nolte who is an outsider to the historical profession, a historical philosopher rather than a historian, who has advanced theories which, as any historian knows, he has essentially been putting forth for twenty years. But it is only now that these views are found to be scandalous. At first, when the *Frankfurter Allgemeine* published Ernst Nolte's theses, there was hardly a reaction. The outrage only broke out when it was realized that Nolte's ideas could be used in the battle against particular government plans, against political positions adopted by the government and against those historical assessments which could be seen as problematical, if not politically counterproductive. But it is not until now that the whole question of the Holocaust has become the actual subject of a debate, the real foundations of which are, I am convinced, quite different.

NICHOLAS HENDERSON: The thought that occurs to me relates to some of the themes of Ralf Dahrendorf's agenda and that is, what is the political relevance at this time of this analysis and acceptance of Germany's past? It seems to me that this issue is not only timely for Germany, but that it is exceedingly timely for other countries as well. Not only do the Germans feel that they want to decide for themselves about their past and relevance to the future, but I think that the circumstances in Europe and in the world make it extremely pertinent that we, the outsiders, should come to a view regarding these questions. Let me explain what I mean. Michael Stürmer referred twice to the changed international circumstances. In considering this question I think we must have in mind how enormous these likely changes are that affect Germany and other people's attitudes towards Germany.

On the horizon now is the likelihood of the removal of all the United States' intermediate nuclear missiles from Europe but also there is a very considerable pressure in the United States for the reduction of conventional forces. These are totally paradoxical things: if you give up the nuclear you ought to increase conventional forces, but that is not the direction in which policy appears to be developing. What is the relevance of this horizon I'm depicting to the question of the nature of Germany's past? If these things occur most people in Europe will deduce that this amounts in some way to a diminution of United States interest in, and possibly support for the Federal Republic. The question is, what is the consequence of that possibility on the minds of German people, this new generation which knows nothing of Hitler and that age? What they come to believe or are taught about their past will have a bearing on what they think the consequences will be of the international changes I have mentioned; likewise what other countries conclude about recent German history will have relevance to the impact they think that such changes may have on German attitudes and policies.

Another remark made by Michael Stürmer interested me. He said, and the point has been reflected in other statements, that Germany needs a national identity which will not be satisfied by membership in NATO, let alone in the European community. Those of us outside, who take an interest in this question, have really to try to understand what is meant by this idea of a national identity. What do the Russians think, what sort of national identity are they prepared to accept on the basis of their interpretation of the German past? I would like someone to clarify for me what form of national identity the Germans have in mind and how this fits in with the needs of the rest of Europe.

HANS MOMMSEN: I think we have very different concepts of national identity in West Germany. On the whole the problem has been blown up by a group of intellectuals and certainly by interested government circles mainly for domestic reasons. There is no programme, even the most radical Pan-Germans, if I may use that term, don't want to change the frontiers. We should not spend so much time talking about this issue. I believe West Germans are in the process of finding their identity. It seems reasonable that they should not have recourse to the Wilhelmine or Bismarckian Empire which has bleak associations for the younger generation, but that they build up an identity on a regional level, that they create a means of identifying with the Federal Republic as a nation whilst not excluding the other part of Germany from that understanding. I think we should look at the origins of the historians' dispute and the polarization around certain historical issues more closely. Before 8 May 1985, I remember, we had a discussion amongst the trade unions about how to deal with that date. At the time nobody anticipated that this anniversary would suddenly become such a big event which would then be connected with the recreation of an extreme historical sensitivity. The historians' dispute is only one factor.

Eberhard Jäckel is right in saying that the younger generation in Germany which did not experience the Nazi period does feel the burden of the Third Reich. They do not go along with manipulated nationalism. The concern of some conservatives or neo-conservatives, shared by some Americans and other foreign observers, regarding the absence in West Germany of a normal nationalism, in the nineteenth century sense, is unfounded. I'm fairly optimistic. We don't need Cassandra-Kohls. I think the historians' dispute occurred in the mid-eighties and not ten years earlier because of a crisis of legitimacy in the party system. In a way, seeking refuge in history is a reflection of this crisis.

HAROLD JAMES: One of the points raised by the timing issue is the question of the disintegration of an American system of hegemony in the 1970s and 1980s. It's a theme that's been taken up here by Carol Gluck, with reference to Japan, by Michael Stürmer and by Sir Nicholas Henderson. It seems to me that there are striking parallels with the 1920s. On the whole one can think of that era as a period of unstable British and American joint-hegemony and that the collapse of Germany at the end of the 1920s and the circumstances of the world economic crisis produced in Germany and elsewhere a striking growth of nationalism.

If one were to look at the world in general in the 1970s and 1980s one would find a similar growth of nationalism. The Japanese example was particularly instructive but we don't need to think of Japan alone in connection with nationalist revivals which pose a danger to world peace. We can think of Ireland and Central America, we can think of South America and of course the Middle East. In this context it seems to me that the story of a possible nationalist revival in Germany, as expressed by alleged attempts at altering views of German history, is very mild indeed. It simply isn't on the scale of the revival of powerful aggressive and destructive nationalism that we see elsewhere in the world.

Indeed, I think one should stress that there is a relative consensus in Germany among the political parties about national responsibility and that, for instance, the CDU has been moving towards accepting a sort of bipartisan version of *Ostpolitik* since the early seventies. We find that in the debates about whether to support Barzel's vote of no confidence against the Brandt government, the disaffection of CDU parliamentarians in that case, we find it in the case of Honecker's visit to West Germany in 1987. This seems to me to be a story of responsibility rather than a story of irresponsibility. This is an important framework for looking at the issues we have been dealing with here. Given the particular difficulties of Germany, given the ambiguities of what is meant by German identity one should be particularly wary of potential dangers. That, I think, has been one of the productive functions of this debate.

JÜRGEN KOCKA: I would like to say something about the need for identity and the possible role of history in fulfilling that need. But let me begin with the *Historikerstreit*. It is important to date the beginning of the dispute in order to be able to assess its meaning. I disagree with Stürmer in that I don't think that Habermas' article started the whole thing off. Maybe Jäckel goes too far when he says that the Bitburg incident marks the beginning, yet Habermas certainly reacted to something. He tried to answer what he perceived as a challenge. This challenge was posed by Nolte's article but also by Hillgruber's writings and Stürmer's speeches and articles. I fully understand Hillgruber saying that he has nothing to do with Nolte's thesis. Michael Stürmer is probably right in stressing that he never took a position akin to Nolte's on the connection between the Bolsheviks and the Nazis and on Weizmann's role. It is true, these three historians vary in their views. Yet they resemble one another in one fundamental respect, and this justified Habermas' linking them: in their writings, all three have tried to interpret our past in a slightly more acceptable, less critical way. This fits into the context of Bitburg, of the discussion about memorials, of several statements by politicians in the electoral campaign. It is therefore not so difficult to understand why this dispute was unleashed at that particular time.

Stürmer's repeated statements, Joachim Fest's arguments, the Kissinger quote – are all part of the same feeling that there is not enough consensus in our society, that we lack sufficient identity, that we are walking on thin ice. The Federal Republic has been seen as an economy in search of becoming a state. I reject this view. We have been a state for a long time, although – fortunately – we are not a great power. After all, we have a liberal constitutional system which has tried successfully to draw conclusions from German history. This represents more than just economic success, it is a good record in liberal terms, in constitutional terms and in terms of many young people identifying with the Federal Republic. I can't see a lack of consensus. As Harold James said, it is remarkable how far the CDU has moved to compromise on certain policies which it opposed fifteen or twenty years ago: *Ostpolitik* is a prime example. One can also think of Habermas and the section of the Left which he stands for. In the sixties there was much more opposition from that side against basic principles of the Federal Republic. Nowadays many of them support the basic principles of the state. We have a great deal of consensus in the Federal Republic. I wonder how those who look at West Germany from the outside view this feeling that there is not enough identity. It is, in my opinion, central to the historians' debate.

MICHAEL STÜRMER: The problem is not identity but orientation.

JÜRGEN KOCKA: In this debate the term 'identity' refers to a collective feeling and awareness which supports consensus, provides for common orientation and strengthens the legitimacy of the system. In other words, 'identity' includes 'orientation'. I am not sure what will happen to the historical profession if this public demand for historians to participate in creating identity grows. I don't want to be polemical, especially not about Nolte in his absence, but I think there are examples of what can happen to history as a science in such cases. It can easily be tempted to violate its standards.

I would like to stress that historians should not overrate themselves. Important sources for collective identity are to be found elsewhere, in the 'efficiency' of a society or a system, not only in economic but also in liberal, constitutional terms, in the ability to create conditions which make life worth living. This may be much more important than certain views of history. I don't think the Federal Republic has the worst record in this field over the last years. We should also not overrate the *Historikerstreit*. We are discussing it here, the media have devoted space to it, but a large majority of historians in West Germany don't care about it at all. Specialist historians are not really interested in the *Historikerstreit*. We know from experience that some issues tend to be blown up for a while and then fade away very quickly. This debate is also a media thing. We should not overrate the importance of what we are discussing here and draw conclusions regarding the stability of the consensus in the Federal Republic of Germany.

EBERHARD JÄCKEL: I was a student in America during the 1952 presidential election campaign and I have never forgotten Adlai Stevensen's slogan: 'Let's talk sense to the American people'. I think it is important for our discussion, for our political culture to speak clearly, to argue rationally and to provide facts to back what is said. I would like to reassure Herr Fest that I never claimed that he tried to rehabilitate the Nazi past. I would appreciate it if he were to prove on what occasion I allegedly said this. I never said it, I never meant it and I would not have proposed to my faculty that he be awarded an honorary doctorate if I ever thought so. I do not think it is right to argue in this way. I said that the statements Fest made in this context had the effect of reducing the relative place of the Nazi past in German public life.

JOACHIM FEST: Herr Jäckel, when you spoke about the Right in the Federal Republic you did not mention me by name, but in your attack you spoke above all of Nolte and myself. If you did not intend to establish a connection by doing so, then your allegation does not make sense, or at any rate I understood nothing of what you said.

EBERHARD JÄCKEL: Surely one can distinguish between the term rehabilitation, that is to say, justification of a regime and the attempt to restrict the public debate about this system without prettifying it or playing it down. But I would like to make two further comments on this topic. Herr Fest now speaks of Nolte's article which appeared in June 1986 as though he had to decide between publishing it or suppressing it. I have never disputed the correctness of your decision in publishing this piece. I have here a speech of mine, which was reprinted in a newspaper, in which I specifically said that in a free society one must be allowed to make statements like Nolte's and Fest's. And I would caution against anyone arguing that it should not be permissible to say such things.

But this is not the problem. The problem is that a few weeks later Fest took up Nolte's arguments and supported them in a much longer article of his own. Again, he had every right to do so. I replied with an essay in which I addressed, in what I believe to have been an unpolemical way, Fest's three arguments against the singularity of the murder of the Jews and opposed them with three counter-arguments. I think it would be of benefit to the political debate in Germany if such arguments were settled. Up until now I have not received a reply to my arguments.

I must make a final comment in answer to a rather outrageous point Hagen Schulze raised. I do not know what the context was, but Schulze mentioned the memorial to the liberation movements of German history in Rastatt. It is a specialist museum and incidentally, President Heinemann whom Schulze alluded to, had no influence on it and neither did I as his advisor. The concept was worked out by the Bundesarchiv (the State archive) without any influence from elsewhere. The reason the Holocaust is not represented in the museum is due to the simple fact – which should be obvious in any rational discussion – that the Holocaust was not part of the liberation movements in German history. It is tantamount to saying that the Cézanne museum is lovely, but what a pity that it does not have any Monets.

MICHAEL STÜRMER: Well, Eberhard Jäckel has convinced us that Good will soon triumph over Evil. He has read one of my editorials in which I used the term *aufrechter Gang* in that meticulous way he reads documents. You don't have to be conservative to read Ernst Bloch and to realize that this was a recognizable or unrecognizable quotation from his work and I see nothing wrong in citing him. Someone might still wish to explain the conspicuous silence which followed, when some of our colleagues stumbled into the pitfall of vanity and ambition, when they had a chance to verify the so-called Hitler diaries. Herr Jäckel might be able to enlighten us.

As to totalitarianism and anti-totalitarianism, the concept goes back even further than Hannah Arendt to Siegmund Neumann, the Chicago sociologist who emigrated to the United States in 1933. The year before he had written a seminal book on German political parties in which he puts communists and Nazis into the same category, the *Absolutistische Integrationspartei*, the absolutist party of integration, not a particularly attractive term, but an interesting concept. Neumann argues that there were similarities between the two at the time of the Hitler-Stalin pact and after the war. It had nothing to do with justifying the Nazis, either before they came to power or afterwards. It had a great deal to do with what a French historian has called *la tentation totalitaire*, the totalitarian temptation of the twentieth century and the striking similarities and differences between the various expressions of totalitarianism. It is a comparative category and scholars like Karl Dietrich Bracher or Hannah Arendt never intended it to serve to justify the atrocities of the Nazis. This is a monstrous allegation.

The Federal Republic rejected both the Nazi past and Stalinism, the basic constitutional law is an expression of this process. It is also an expression of a certain interpretation of history, in the sense that all the constructive and acceptable aspects of German history were rescued: federalism, the state of law, the welfare state, parliamentarianism, universal suffrage. The nasty elements, the temptations were rejected. To some extent this interpretation of history embodied in the Basic Law has, I feel, receded into the background during the past fifteen or twenty years. I am thinking of the attack on the market economy, which to my mind represents an attack on pluralism because you can't have pluralism unless you have a pluralistic economy; I am thinking of the attack on the values of the *Verfassungsstaat*, the constitutional state – why not denounce it as a 'formal democracy', or 'the system'? Why not try and see how far it will bear bending the rules of the game? We have seen all this over the last twenty years, and we are seeing it today.

Someone has rightly asked what this 'identity' is of which we constantly speak. I don't find the term particularly helpful. I did not invent it, it is there, and if I could eliminate it, I would willingly do so. I would rather speak about long-term orientations concerning the past, the present and the future.

Of course every historian is aware that his assumptions about the future affect his perception of the past. And in fact certain interpretations are slowly changing. How could it be otherwise? If the real world changes, this affects historiography just as it affects other fields. Since the idea of a growth economy and of more and cheaper energy has fallen on hard times, the historical interpretation of progress built on growth and expansion is bound to suffer. At the same time, if the world is changing in economic and strategic terms, if the entire configuration is rearranged, it is almost inevitable that historians, among others, should start asking themselves about the rules of the new game, or of the old one.

A certain change in those basic assumptions is reflected in my own academic biography. I began as a constitutional historian, wrote some books on eighteenth century culture, social history, artisans and then found the question raised by the present changes in international affairs in general, and in Central Europe in particular, equally important.

I would now like to reply to Sir Nicholas Henderson who asked what really is at stake. The political consensus in the Federal Republic still comprises *Deutschlandpolitik* and *Ostpolitik*. Nothing much has changed here. I happen to be one of the signatories of the proclamation made in 1972 by German historians offering the government and parliament advice on *Deutschlandpolitik*. It was all a little ridiculous, but we felt very important at the time. Now I happen to be among those who helped shape the continuity of *Deutschlandpolitik* in and after 1982. The real break in *Deutschlandpolitik* occurred not when Kohl took over from Schmidt, but when Schmidt succeeded Brandt. I think most politicians in the Federal Republic accept what's being done in that field today as something with which they are broadly in agreement.

Matters are more difficult when it comes to the Atlantic orientation. There is a feeling of bitterness in certain quarters who allege that Germany is being culturally colonized by the United States. I don't want to sound polemical and name those who argue this case, but there are prominent figures among them. Others think that if the Atlantic system were to break down, the European system would break down as well, and Germany would be left with an uncertain destiny. Despite their different political backgrounds, Zbigniew Brzezinski and Henry Kissinger have used the same term for what they perceive as the alternative to Atlanticism, and that is 'self-finlandization'. I think it is a misleading term but it indicates a direction. There is also much debate about putting Europe, or *Mitteleuropa* first, which implies a different set of values. In domestic politics there is a fundamental debate between 'liberal' democracy based on the market economy and 'socialist' democracy, to identify the most important cleavage. When it comes to Nazism, there is no real difference between one side and the other in their condemnation of the horrors of the regime. The difference lies in the context and in the long-term explanation. This brings us back to the anti-totalitarian interpretation of Nazism embodied in the constitutional law, and to what was referred to as 'anti-fascism' in 1945, was known by this term before then and has been ever since. Among the many cleavages this is probably the most important one. The Germans will have to find their way through them.

In my opinion identity doesn't mean that one could or should be allowed to say: 'This is how you ought to define yourself.' It is the task of historians to understand the broad questions that present themselves as a change of paradigm, to grasp them in their particular intellectual and academic way. If they fail, they will lose their public and neglect an important function of academic discourse. We are not called upon to provide answers for politicians, but to provide an intellectual and possibly a broader public with matter for reflection. No more and no less. I sympathize with what Jürgen Kocka said. There is a hopeful side to which I alluded; but I also see the dark side of a nation which is fundamentally unsure about its future, its role in the world, its own character. When Helmut Schmidt says that Germans are a nation at risk I take that seriously. I try to reflect this not only in my more popular writing but in the academic work I am engaged in. There is a kind of dialogue between academics and the general public; the work of some historians tends to reflect one part of this dialogue while mine tends to reflect the other. I think we ought to re-establish some civilized rules of play because there is a very real debate which will continue regardless of whether German historians take part in it or not. Without them it might have less of a historical orientation.

RALF DAHRENDORF: The latter part of the discussion has taken a different course from the one I had anticipated. Nevertheless, it was obviously necessary. It shows that there are undercurrents which run very deep and which make one wonder whether rational discourse as advocated by Joachim Fest – and I share his preference for a straightforward eighteenth century notion of enlightenment which has not gone through the filter of Hegel and others – is possible under these circumstances. Perhaps we should accept that it is not, and turn instead to issues which can be discussed, such as those raised by Sir Nicholas Henderson and others about the attempt to make some sense of history in a changed environment with a view to the future. In my opinion this changed environment makes it unfitting to focus too much on one's navel. Indeed, it is one of the great risks of today that too many countries are looking inward rather than outward and are overly concerned with matters which they believe concern them alone. I very much hope Germany will continue to be part of an international scene which accepts interdependence, multilaterism and that it continues to contribute to a system which, as Sir Nicholas Henderson, Carol Gluck and others have pointed out, has changed since the immediate post-war period. I would therefore appeal to you not to return to questions which will remain unsolved.

LORD WEIDENFELD: The observation I wanted to make has been partly pre-empted by Michael Stürmer and Jürgen Kocka. I think this meeting may have paid more handsome tribute to the real achievement of the Federal Republic and the German people in the past forty years. I don't mean only the economic progress, I mean the political, intellectual and moral contribution. It is an enormous achievement to have built a politically functioning democracy in forty years. A certain intellectual xenophilia is very specific to the Federal Republic, I can say this from my professional experience as a publisher who has visited the Frankfurt Book Fair for forty years and who deals with German colleagues, and there are also statistics which show that more works are translated from other languages in Germany than anywhere else.

I do not need to talk about the richness and pluralism of cultural life in the Federal Republic. But I must pay tribute to the very high humanitarian and moral standard of German policies with regard to the Third World, to foreign aid. As a Jew and a politically active Zionist I want to state categorically that after the United States the Federal Republic is Israel's greatest friend. Other countries have intermittently made great contributions to Israel, but the contribution of people like Heuss, Adenauer, Weizsäcker have been consistent. They rank amongst the most active supporters and friends of the Jewish people. I don't want to minimize the role of people like Schumacher, Brandt and Schmidt, but, although I will not condone certain lapses of taste, I must also emphasize that the first German chancellor to visit Israel was Helmut Kohl. He may not have behaved as tactfully as he might in Israel but this was not through illwill, he may have been badly advised.

The controversial Franz Josef Strauß also proved himself a most effective friend of Israel's in an hour of need. In the last few days before the Six Day War, when Nasser had closed the straights and the United Nations withdrew and there was justified fear that chemical and gas warfare might be employed by an unscrupulous foe, it was Strauß who used his influence on the coalition government to get gas masks for the defenders of Tel Aviv, it was he who saw to it that the supply was not stopped by Fanfani on the way.

I would like to think that the sum total of these achievements should constitute a good foundation for a national identity or for national self-confidence upon which the Federal Republic can build further. Whilst by no means belittling the importance of scholarly research into the Nazi period and the uniquely dastardly deeds of the regime, I also see it as the duty and as a great challenge and opportunity for historians to give a new generation a sense of its own worth, of its own achievements and of the strength of German history and culture. I have recently visited East Germany. However sinister the motive, I found the reconstruction of the past, the sense of there having been a German history, a German tradition, quite admirable. I think the German historian should concentrate on creating a new self-confidence, this new sense of self-esteem which Germany needs. We need Germany in the West, we need Germany everywhere and those who suffered most from Adolf Hitler's Germany need the new Germany most of all.

RALF DAHRENDORF: We began with what will inevitably come to be called the *Historikerstreit*. I think each one of us will have to make up his or her own mind in assessing the issues, the different positions. It will remain to be seen whether this is an episode which is now over, or whether this is the beginning of a long drawn out discussion consisting of a variety of different arguments, as someone has suggested.

I remain puzzled about the precise subject of this dispute. Of course we have all given thought to the reasons for the emotional intensity of the debate. I wonder what it springs from and whilst I don't have an answer, it struck me – this may or may not be relevant – that there is a tendency on the part of the participants to put the other side into categories which it does not accept. So one gets overt professions of common values, orientations and interests, and then underneath imputations to this or that group; there don't seem to be any real categories in which people see themselves. If one were to say to Irving Kristol or to Norman Podhoretz, you wretched neo-conservatives, they would have something to say about the wretched, but they would accept being called neo-conservatives; in fact, they would make a point of explaining their views in no uncertain terms.

The participants of this debate react differently, they do not want to be put in categories, and yet categories keep cropping up for polemical purposes. The only explanation I can think of for the emotional intensity is that we are probably experiencing some form of rearrangement or realignment of intellectual groupings, whose outcome is as yet uncertain. This process may well take some time. I hope it will not go on in quite the same style, because I do not believe labelling people adds much to developing orientations for the future. I hope, however, that we can discuss history and politics without reiterating the differences which became apparent earlier on and can try to make sense of this complicated and important relationship between the two.

Our second subject was an attempt at putting the German situation in perspective. I am grateful to Robert Conquest and Carol Gluck. They have added a dimension to this conference by showing that concern with history is not confined to Germany and that the writing and re-writing of history has a topical and in many cases a political function in other countries as well. I have certainly been confirmed in my view that of all the issues we have been confronted with, the Soviet issue of dealing with history is easily the most serious. The story which Robert Conquest told us about the difficulty of writing history at all, about the archives, about official and unofficial truth, is, I suspect, much more dramatic and serious than either the German *Historikerstreit* or the curious solidarity marches of various views in Japan.

We then touched indirectly on the vexing question of why some issues, especially the Holocaust and the German Nazi past came to the fore in the past few years in the way they did, why the *Historikerstreit* took place now. In the past Germany had a number of public figures, such as Austria has today in Waldheim, who were involved with the Nazis and did not always find it easy to come to terms with their own past, but there wasn't much discussion then, whereas today, those who rise to prominent positions are subjected to international scrutiny.

I don't want to reopen the discussion about the origins of the historians' dispute, but let me just remind you of one or two points that were made. Some participants argued in almost universal terms. There was reference to the forty year theme in the Bible. It was suggested that perhaps forty years is a long enough period for certain memories to recur. Others have argued in general terms and spoken about generation changes, that those who remember the thirties and forties are getting on in age, that a new generation is taking over and that something is happening at this point of transition, something which was, or was not, bound to happen at that stage. Others have pointed to the changes in the international scene, to a world which can no longer rely on the institutions of the immediate post-war order. They have pointed to a world of shifting relationships where all those concerned are forced to re-examine their links with others and to re-examine the path they are treading, a process which may lead to a redefinition or reinvigoration of some of the existing institutions like NATO. Several participants referred to what may be called the lessons of the 1970s, the end of the notion of progress or rather, if that is an overstatement, the fact that progress was no longer taken as a matter of course, that there were doubts in the continuation of certain trends, economic or otherwise which relied on the past. And it has been argued that these doubts may have brought about a desire to look back to where one came from and to re-open dossiers which seemed closed for some time.

I have taken these points from my notes on the discussion. Most of them need not only apply to Germany but to many countries. A number of specifically German reasons were also given for the debate occurring when it did. Certain publications, conferences and the German federal election in January 1987 were mentioned, as were the ways in which Germans have tried to come to terms with their past and the various interpretations of it. That's quite a hodge podge. I am not sure it adds up to a clear explanation of the issue of timing. I for one would like to read a few articles here and there in the foreseeable future about this point because it may be one of the clues, not only to the intensity of the debate but also to the question of where it is likely to lead us.

We now move on to our last question. I have called it the relationship between history and politics, a fairly bland description. I hope we will have an intense but calm discussion on this key subject. Let me call first on Gordon Craig and then on Wolfgang Mommsen.

GORDON CRAIG: Jürgen Kocka has said that we should be well-advised not to take the *Historikerstreit* too seriously. I think that I would go a step further and say that we should not take *ourselves* too seriously, and in saying this I refer not only to my German colleagues but to American historians as well. We are not really very important people; we do not enjoy much prestige in our societies; and our political influence, never very great in recent times, is rapidly approaching the vanishing point. Worse, this is all our own fault. In the pluralistic, free-market society, we have been the least constrained, the most self-indulgent of beneficiaries. We have squandered our responsibilities and forfeited the respect of those whom it was our duty to serve.

It is not difficult to support these charges.

Item. It must be more than thirty years now since Lord Dacre delivered a lecture in Oxford that I have never forgotten. In it he elaborated on the difference between humane and scientific studies, arguing that, unlike the scientific or useful studies, the humanities had no very direct claim upon society and that, if they had any legitimacy at all, it was derived from their contact with, and their services to, the lay public. I was greatly moved by this lecture, which I took to be a warning to historians. If it was that, it was largely disregarded. It is well known that academic historians have long since given up writing for the lay public. Indeed, they have so neglected the arts of intelligibility and clarity of style that most of them are incapable of doing so. They write for each other, and they are much more concerned about being quoted correctly by their colleagues than about being understood by a wider public. In our debates during these last two days, we have had some evidence of this.

Item. We have (this is certainly true of my own country, and I suspect it is not without truth in Germany also) stood idly by as historical instruction has been virtually eliminated from the curriculum of the lower schools and gravely weakened in the secondary ones. In the last few weeks, a report of the National Council on Education has revealed the appalling state of historical knowledge on the part of high school juniors and seniors in the United States, large numbers of whom cannot identify the Hoover whose name stands on the Hoover Dam, have no idea who George Catlett Marshall may have been, and cannot come within 50 years of guessing the dates of the Civil War, let alone recognize the relationship between that conflict and the emancipation of the slaves. This is the result of the failure of the most important historians in the profession to interest themselves even minimally in what goes on in the American school system. It is the result of a shameful – all the more shameful because thoughtless, feckless – capitulation to Schools of Education and State School Boards.

Item. In a world in which, as Sir Nicholas Henderson told us yesterday, great changes impend that may well determine and will certainly influence the future of national states, academic historians have practically stopped studying, writing about or teaching diplomatic and military history and the history of inter-national relations. In the welter of courses on economic and social history, regional history, *Alltagsgeschichte*, women's history, psychohistory, Holocaust history (which has become a growth industry in the United States), and other specialities that fill the history curricula of major universities, it is difficult to find comprehensive lecture courses, colloquia or seminars on the history of foreign relations since the Thirty Years War or of international organization since the Congress of Vienna, or even of the diplomacy of the bipolar world that has existed since 1949. Many universities have no diplomatic historians or specialists on international affairs in their history departments, although until the year 1945 this was the area in which a department's most distinguished members were generally to be found. About four years ago, in an address to the general meeting of the American Historical Association in Washington, DC, I pointed out that in the last seven meetings of the Association there had been an average of only 5 out of 128 sessions devoted to the study·of international relations in any of its forms. I suggested that in a country that claimed to be a Superpower and whose foreign policy needed all the help that it could get, this was not good enough, and I urged that, since there was abundant evidence that our students were interested in international subjects, we should do something to satisfy that need. The response to that appeal has been negligible, which means that most of our students graduate without any systematic knowledge of world politics and that those among them who become school teachers carry their ignorance with them to edify their pupils.

If academic historians neglect these constituencies, who supplies the historical needs of the great public? As far as the cultivated lay reading public is concerned, we are fortunate in possessing in people like Joachim Fest and Barbara Tuchman and Sebastian Haffner supremely gifted non-academic historians who write about serious subjects for them. We also have thousands of popularizers who write tendentious and highly romanticized history and whose influence is not so healthy.

But the greater part of historical instruction of the popular masses is provided, as Carol Gluck pointed out yesterday, by the politicians and the manipulators of the public memory. These are people who often have contempt for professional historians and for the canons of the historical craft. They are great *users* of history for their own ends, and adroit in finding spurious historical justification for their hidden agenda, but they are often clumsy to the point of maladroitness in the presentation of their historical extravaganza. These are the perpetrators of fiascos like Bitburg and the official Japanese visit to the shrines of the war criminals. These are the people responsible for President Reagan's curious idea of celebrating the 200th anniversary of the US Constitution, that marvellous instrument that has proven itself to be adaptable to all of the problems of modern industrial society, by nominating as Justice to the Supreme Court a man who is a strict constructionist and appears to believe that the Constitution cannot be used to invalidate laws that violate human and social rights unless this can be shown to have been the specific intent of the framers.

To allow politicians to determine the nature of the history that is communicated one way or another to the mass of people is perilous because politicians suffer from all of what I once called the 'dangers of historical thinking', and from three of these dangers most of all:

1: the use of the false analogy. Thus, in the years when the Cold War was at its height, and particularly during the Vietnam War, they were prone to what can be called the Munich Syndrome and constantly argued, on the basis of a loose and generalized view of the consequences of the Munich Conference of 1938, that compromises and concessions were always ruinous in their consequences and that there was no substitute for complete victory;

2: the use of dialectical and other patterns of history to justify one's course. Thus, in the days of Presidents Truman and Kennedy, members of the Policy Planning Staff were great readers of Thucydides' *History of the Peloponnesian War* and were always explaining that we were Athens and they were Sparta (although one might have thought that this was an analogy that was neither flattering nor encouraging) and that we must be prepared to wage our conflict with the same unconditionality, and the same brutal disregard for those who did not wish to become involved, as those earlier adversaries, for history demanded it. Thus, the United States, the greatest of neutrals in the nineteenth century, became contemptuous of neutral rights and neutrals in the Cold War. We did not actually destroy the citizens of Melos, but sometimes we talked as if we wanted to.

3: the tendency (shared unfortunately by many historians) to overvalue continuity at the expense of change. This is one of the reasons why we are always being surprised in our foreign policy and forced into a reactive stance.

In their more elevated moments, historians like to think of themselves as protectors of the collective memory, charged – as Thomas Nipperdey wrote not so long ago – with the task of 'illuminating our recollection of the past and protecting it from legends and manipulations'. They take pride in the thought that they are the people best endowed to demonstrate what human beings are capable of by showing what they have been and have done, and that in this way they can help the present generation to understand both its limitations and its possibilities. When I am in an optimistic mood, I share this rather idealized view of our special calling, but I am never so optimistic that I do not remember that we cannot fulfil this noble function unless we can persuade someone to take us seriously.

We shall hardly get a hearing from the politicians, who are not at the moment very interested in anything we have to say. Some years ago I read in the newspapers that Senator Richard Lugar was heading a congressional committee to draw up a list of national priorities. I had met Lugar, and so I wrote to him and suggested that his committee might invite the President and the President-Elect of the American Historical Association to testify before it. Senator Lugar answered that they had a very full schedule and that he doubted whether that could be arranged. Nor was it.

In June of this year, Professor Fritz Stern gave an address before the Bundestag in Bonn in commemoration of the East German rising of 17 June 1953. When he pointed out that the rising was not in any way a demonstration in favour of reunification and went on to say that 'undivided Germany had brought unspeakable misfortune to other peoples and to itself', adding that the current debate in the Federal Republic over the German past was a kind of seismograph of German consciousness, which was causing much concern abroad about the 'restless Germans', there was a storm of protest, although those things were indubitably true, or perhaps *because* they were true and the politicians did not want to be told the truth by a historian qualified to report it.

If historians wish to have any influence on politics, they must, it seems to me, go back to the true source of their strength. They must follow the advice of Jakob Burckhardt, who once said – it was in the introduction of his book on the age of Constantine – that he was not interested in writing books for the guild, books that would end up on the lower shelves of university libraries, but books that would be read, and whenever possible bought, by ordinary readers. We must go back to the lay public from whom our legitimacy is derived, and hope that our writings for them will help them exert a healthy influence upon policy-making that is the hallmark of a sound democracy. That is the natural way, and the most effective way, for the historian to influence politics. And, while we are turning our attention, and the focus of our work, back to the lay public, we should try to do something about the deplorable state of historical instruction in the schools and the lack of emphasis upon the history of world politics and foreign relations in our university curricula. There have been moments during this doubtless interesting and valuable discussion when I have had a feeling of airlessness and wished the windows could be opened. There is a great big world out there, and it deserves our earnest attention.

WOLFGANG MOMMSEN: Professor Craig's comments are rather pessimistic. I tend to strike a more positive note, but that may just be a matter of age.

The debate about 'The Germans and Their Past' touches upon a most fundamental issue: the relationship of history and politics. It may safely be said that most, if not all parties involved in the *Historikerstreit* are agreed on one thing, and that is that history matters, that *Geschichtsbilder*, images of the past, are powerful. It is assumed that notions about the past can substantially influence the political orientation of groups and individuals, and exercise a strong influence on the course of events, if not in the short, then in the long run. This, I presume, was a motive for most of those who took part in this debate, though perhaps not everybody was aware of this aspect to the same degree. It was argued during the early stages of the debate that the controversy had been launched for political reasons only, but that it was in fact a non-issue. I believe that the course of the debate has demonstrated that this position is not tenable. The *Historikerstreit* is about fundamental differences in the interpretation of recent German history which, so it is assumed, have considerable political ramifications.

I am not concerned here with the question of whether or to what extent any of these positions in the debate are correct, but rather with the fundamental assumption about the function of history, that being that historical notions, if held by substantial social groups, may have a direct impact on the course of historical events. I believe that history does matter, or, to put it in another way, that historical consciousness is an important factor in determining the political orientation of individuals and peoples. Having said this, I would like to suggest caution about assuming a direct link between historical consciousness and political convictions, let alone political action.

In a way, historical consciousness is in itself largely conditioned by a given social situation. Historians are children of their own time; they articulate rather than create fundamental assumptions about the past held by specific social groups in particular historical constellations. [In the case of the *Historikerstreit* I would have thought that the new lines of interpretation which have come to the fore recently are a reaction to underlying changes in the mentality of West Germans.]

Historians should perhaps not overrate their role in forming public consciousness even in matters directly related to the interpretation of history. Even so, the interpretations which historians give to certain segments of history may not only reflect a particular trend, but strengthen it. This can have considerable political consequences and it therefore imposes a great moral responsibility on historians; they should be aware of what they are doing.

I would like to illustrate my point by referring to a number of historical examples other than the *Historikerstreit*.

A. It is well known that the Borussian interpretation of German History which was established and gradually developed by a number of eminent German historians of National Liberal allegiance helped to bring about and, in time, stabilize the semi-constitutional system created by Bismarck in 1867–71; the national consensus in Imperial Germany rested on a particular image of the past to which professional historians had contributed a great deal. It is obvious today that this image was partly false. Besides it encompasses many undesirable elements, regarding, for instance, the attitude towards national minorities including the Jews. Treitschke's plea for the complete assimilation of the Jews corresponded with an integralist notion of the nation state, embedded in a particular understanding of German history. Theodor Mommsen on the other hand argued against this from the vantage point of a liberal notion of the nation state. It was a bitter argument which also had a personal dimension. Theodor Mommsen refused to sit next to Treitschke in the Prussian Academy of Sciences.

B. The Weimar Republic stood no real chance of winning through, given the fact that the educated classes steadfastly refused to revise their notion of recent German history, and to adjust their *Geschichtsbild* to the democratic ideals embodied in the Weimar constitution. Instead, Imperial Germany was seen as the yardstick of normality, and the contemporary state of affairs described as a sad aberration from the normal path of German history.

C. The Fischer-Debate in the early 1960s was, in a way, a controversy which ought to have been conducted in the 1920s. It was a symptom of a time-lag in the development of German historical thought compared with the development of Western historical thought. At the same time it was a bitter controversy about what and how much had been wrong with the Germans and with German political institutions in Imperial Germany and later.

D. To take an example from a non-German context, one might think of the so-called Whig interpretation of history. People have become disenchanted with it today. But during the nineteenth century a society in which the aristocratic elite was able to hold on to political control for a very long time by integrating some segments of the rising middle classes into their ranks used the Whig interpretation of history as a source of legitimacy. This notion of the past strengthened the established order. At the same time it could be used as historical evidence to justify gradual reform.

E. A more recent example, already alluded to by Lord Annan, is the so-called 'Standard of Living Debate' in Britain conducted in the 1960s and 1970s, with Eric Hobsbawm as the spokesman for the so-called 'Pessimists' and Hartwell representing the 'Optimists'. It was about whether early industrialization had led to a further decline in the living standards of the working classes or not. This bitter controversy reflected a notion of guilt about the treatment of the working classes in the nineteenth century which served to underpin the Keynesian welfare policies of the 1960s.

The political function of images of the past (whether people believe in them and/or whether they are propagated by political elitists or adopted by underprivileged groups like the working class who – on the European continent at any rate – developed their own partly realistic, partly utopian notion of history) seems obvious to me. They have always served political purposes of various kinds, be they subconscious or, as was usually the case, calculated. However, it is worth asking when and under which conditions they tended to be politically effective, and/or, perhaps, whether they had positive or negative effects. The latter question can no longer be answered without imposing values; it requires taking a definite position within the time-sequence of history.

In this context the degree to which interpretations of the past are controlled by empirical evidence or not is of considerable momentum. Besides, it is important to see to what extent such interpretations deviate from historical reality at any given moment. However, all interpretations of the past contain a utopian element inasmuch as they are structured not only by our knowledge of the past, but by hopes and expectations about the future.

This meta-scientific aspect of historical knowledge cannot be overcome even by the most erudite historical scholarship. Historical knowledge is perspectival in nature, and different perspectives are conditioned by different political persuasions. Conversely, notions about certain segments of the past which are thought to be meaningful when seen from a given political vantage point, may corroborate, however indirectly, certain political creeds or political positions, or, conversely, undermine them.

Rational debate based upon a full account of all available evidence may help to clarify the issues, but it will never suffice to confirm or falsify underlying assumptions of a political nature. This is only possible if mutually antagonistic positions are equally respected, however abominable they may seem to be.

Max Weber once said that it is not ideas, but 'ideal and material interests' that determine the course of history. But images operate like 'switchmen', *Weichenstellungen*, in determining the direction in which a social system may develop. This applies in particular to images of the past. For this reason it makes sense to discuss the potential rights and wrongs of competing interpretations of history, both as regards their factual accuracy, and their respective perspectival positions. This discussion may not necessarily result in achieving consensus – indeed, this is highly improbable – but it may lead to a critical assessment of the different positions in the light of the ultimate cultural values at stake.

Images of the past are not necessarily linked to historiography; on the contrary, they may present themselves in the form of altogether a-historical notions about social change and the ideal social order. The extent to which political consciousness is explicitly determined by historical notions, let alone by professional historical scholarship, is itself conditioned by historical factors and subject to historical change. The post-war situation in Europe was determined by a state of affairs where history was far less important than social-scientific assumptions of a very general kind. The dominant creed of the day was neo-liberalism, with its emphasis on the initiative of the individual and on the market economy, blended with a Keynesian philosophy of full employment. Its political corollary was the theory of Totalitarianism which emphasized the dichotomy between the almighty state often associated with populist mass policies, and the individual. This philosophy was tantamount to a partial theory of history, but it was formulated by political scientists and sociologists in a primarily dogmatic way; professional historians had little to do with it. It was indirectly strengthened by the polarization between the two world systems and by an outstanding economic recovery; it was curiously static in nature, although it represented a particular image of the past; it worked on the assumption that the great problems of the past were solved once and for all; it assumed that a new, post-ideological age of gradual reform and piecemeal engineering was *ante portas*.

Since the 1970s this philosophy has been progressively eroded. The theory of Totalitarianism was largely falsified, as it had been based on wrong empirical assumptions about the nature of the National Socialist governmental system. More importantly, the historical conditions which gave plausibility to the postulates of neo-liberalism were gradually withering away. The sharp ideological differences between the capitalist and Marxist-Leninist systems gradually weakened. The antagonism between the superpowers gave way to an era of détente. The period of continuous economic growth came to a halt, and the belief in the possibility of controlling national economies with Keynesian techniques was shattered. Confidence in the automatic functioning of the technological progress gave way to widespread disorientation. As the future had become progressively more uncertain, people once again became interested in history, especially their own national histories, in search of orientation. This partly explains the renewed interest in what is now called the quest for 'national identity'. It remains to be seen whether the historical profession will live up to the expectations of the general public or whether the task will prove too big for it.

LORD ANNAN: I would like to say something about British historians as distinct from what Gordon Craig was saying about America. I am no longer a professional historian, having deserted my profession for academic administration. But in a way I have, over the years, been, like George Weidenfeld, an impresario for history in the sense that if you are running a university, you spend a great deal of time trying to find out who the best historians in a particular field are when a particular appointment has to be made. I have a different impression about the state of history and its popularity in Britain from Gordon Craig. Of course we have our pedants among our academic colleagues, indeed in that inaugural lecture of Hugh Trevor-Roper's which Gordon Craig referred to, I seem to recollect that Trevor-Roper had some rather harsh things to say about medieval historians in Britain whom he accused of editing the laundry lists of nunneries. Without such pedantry none of us could possibly reinterpret history, because it is through the analysis of new evidence that our interpretations of history change. So I don't blame some of my colleagues too much for writing articles, indeed books, which will never be read by the general public.

The question is, are there those who do more than that? I think in Britain this has been so. Indeed, I would say that there has never been a time where there was more 'haute vulgarisation' of history, partly by amateurs like Barbara Tuchman but also by our leading historians in Britain. We need only look around us. There is Hugh Trevor-Roper, there might be, if he were not ill these days, A. J. P. Taylor*. There is Jack Plumb, or Keith Thomas, there is J. H. Elliott, the interpreter of Spain, there was Moses Finlay, the ancient historian. There are Eric Hobsbawm, E. P. Thompson, Asa Briggs, Peter Brown, Geoffrey Best, and many more. All these are names which are well known to the reading public in Britain today. Indeed, even when it comes to such an esoteric subject as the history of ideas, Isaiah Berlin is a household name in Britain, though he may not like that as a description of himself. Take the history of art. There has never been a greater explosion in this field in Britain than in recent times. This has been achieved partly by the great refugees from Hitler's Germany. To them we owe an unparalleled debt. But there are Britons now who are masters of this specialized subject. Kenneth Clark was not an academic, but I hope no one would suggest that he was not a scholar. Perhaps no other scholar could have written the book he wrote called *The Nude*.

What I think has challenged the prestige of history is the pretensions of the social sciences. The social sciences have seduced the allegiance of the young from history. The young have been impressed – too much in my view – by the pretensions of social scientists that their subject gives a truer picture of society, a more scientific interpretation of society and that this picture is more relevant to our times. Then there is the de-personalization of the way in which we look at society, which has received its greatest impetus from Braudel and the Annales school in Paris. I think that it is somewhere after page 479 of volume one in Braudel's *History of the Mediterranean in the Age of Phillip II* that the king is first mentioned. It is, as we all know, a remarkable analysis of the impersonal forces of history.

There has been a reaction among the general public in Britain against Braudel's de-personalization of history. There has been a

---

* A. J. P. Taylor died in September 1990.

phenomenal explosion in biography. Biographies pour from the press, sometimes of course feeble and sensationalized biographies but many of them well-researched, scholarly works which are replacing, as it were, what historians have drained out of history. I think it is true, however, that political history per se has been in decline. Here, as in many points, I am in agreement with what Professor Craig said. This decline is partly due to the enormous stress on social history, on the analysis of the impersonal forces in history. The political history of countries is no longer as popular as it once was. Here the villain of the piece has been, in my view, Herbert Butterfield with his attack on the Whig interpretation of history. In one sense we cannot ignore what Butterfield said. It is true that one must study the past for its own sake and interpret it in its own terms. Nevertheless, it is Butterfield's attack on trying to make sense of the present by what has happened in the past which has eliminated from history so much of its importance in the minds of the young.

I go along with Professor Craig when he says the disaster which has struck our schools in this respect is enormous. Much less history is done in schools. This is partly due to the proliferation of subjects all of which have a claim to importance. This has also had a great effect on the numbers of students reading history at university. Time and again you find that the ones who would have read history in the 1930s read the social sciences today.

These are some of the reasons why I think history as a force in the politics of our country has declined. Nevertheless, there is a change coming about. I notice for example in the work of Norman Stone that there are people writing today who are very anxious to show their orientation in the present by the way they treat the past. I think it may well be that we shall see a revival of political history, history as having effect on politics.

ROBERT CONQUEST: Noel Annan has pre-empted me a little. I was going to denounce political science more than social science: but I think I can continue on those lines by saying something about the nature of the history which enters, in a very general sense, national consciousness. I think Wolfgang Mommsen is right about the Whig interpretation of history. It really did infiltrate the population. Even now you find people saying, 'It's a free country, isn't it?' They don't say it's a democracy, they have got the old Whig notion of liberty, of rights, rather than political democracy. And, I think, this is, in a general sense, both historically sound and politically healthy. Such public feeling has traditionally come not only through well written or best selling histories but also through historical novels like Thomas Keneally's new book *The Playmaker*. I'm sure these contribute. There is a sort of border line in which history, to use a horrid word, 'interfaces' with the population. I think it is most important that that should be so.

I regard myself as an Anglo-American historian and in spite of the disasters which Gordon Craig has rightly mentioned, I don't find that there is much resistance to reading history. Books sell by the tens of thousands in America – perhaps less than in England – and the situation is not quite as disastrous at this level as it is in the universities and schools. But it is true that a hundred thousand copies of a general history does not balance ten million illiterate graduates.

I was much impressed by Carol Gluck's paper on Japan. I learned a great deal from it and it made me reconsider a few points about the Soviet experience, about what is happening in the Soviet Union now. Historians have been trying to exert pressure for twenty years or more. The ground has been prepared by dissidents, by underground history and foreign radio, and the intellectual world was ready for it. Now it has been allowed to come up because it has been recognized on all levels that the system isn't working and something must be done. As a very rough parallel, I regard the Soviet Union to be in the same condition as France in about 1780, a condition where not only the intellectuals have given up on the system but even the ruling class know that something is wrong and they appoint their Turgots to try and save the situation. But what happens after that is another matter.

The other point about the Soviet Union is that there are very large chunks of history to be coped with. The regime now only accepts Lenin and Khrushchev as legitimate rulers, and if you count the Gorbachev period, you end up officially with about twenty years of good history and fifty years of bad – in two bursts, the Stalin period and the Brezhnev period. The difference between the Soviet Union and Japan and Germany of course, is that the Soviets had a war during the bad period and they won it; 1941–5 is seen as being all right. This is difficult to handle. But the Soviets are attacking Stalin and, curiously, they are now attacking him on his war record. One would think that they'd avoid that, but they are taking him on instead. Nevertheless, the fact that the Soviets went through a heroic period from their point of view under what was an unheroic regime at home, presents a curious problem. The other difference is that mass guilt does not really arise because generally speaking the Soviet people do not feel themselves responsible, nor do the intellectuals. It is the Party which has to face history; and this aspect distinguishes the Soviet Union from Germany, where the people were involved more directly or organizationally at least in the mistakes and have to face what they did. Again, the Germans were not the direct, major victims of Hitlerism, while the Russians, Ukrainians and so on were the direct, major victims of Stalinism.

I have some difficulty with not using the word totalitarian. I don't think one wants 'models', which I regard as mere imports from political science. But the word totalitarian does seem to me to mean something quite useful. I don't want to go into it – I think Giovanni Sartori's new book, or rather the new version of his old book, covers everything that need be said and Kolakowsky has also written interestingly on this subject of late (making clear that the detailed 'efficiency' of the machine is not the point, but rather its ability to crush society). But I think if one starts saying the word isn't of any use when drawing parallels, one is confusing the issue. To say that Hitler and Stalin can both be described as totalitarian does not mean that their crimes are the same, any more than it means criminal A has committed the same crimes as criminal B if you use the word criminal. And the totalitarian idea, the notion of a radical ideology transcending any moral principles and the ability through a fully centralized one party mechanism to put highly specific phantasies into action, are common to the Nazi and Soviet experience. I find it very difficult to see how anyone can be anti-Hitler without being anti-Stalin; indeed, I would say that anyone who is not anti-Stalinist is not really anti-Hitlerist either. The notion that they compete for condemnation seems to me to be absolute nonsense.

I think we have perhaps been exaggeratedly Germanocentric at this conference. There is a larger perspective and I think it is a mistake to try and cut out the existence of Stalin. Of course the Japanese experience is also relevant. I don't see how one can be a historian of Hitlerism without being, to some extent at least, a historian of Stalinism, as well as taking into account all the other phenomena in the world. One has to see the context in which Nazism took place.

FELIX GILBERT: I only really have two questions. The first one concerns the problem which Gordon Craig raised about the decline in influence of history. Lord Annan has spoken about it in connection with England, I would like to look at the German aspect. I usually visit Germany once or twice a year and I then spend a day in one of the big bookshops to see what has come out. I must say that I am always astounded by the number of books which have appeared in the five or six months since I last came. There's Nipperdey and then there's Stürmer's *Das Ruhelose Reich*, there's the big DVA series edited by Eschenburg and Bracher about the history of the Federal Republic and so on. Each of these books is at least 600–800 pages long. In former years nobody would have read such lengthy books. What does this mean? Do the Germans really want to be informed about what happened in the past? What is the reason for the huge amount of historical books produced in Germany?

I would like to link this question with another one. Has a change taken place in Germany and perhaps in the world in general in the relationship between the general public and history? History used to be scholarship. Now it seems to be addressing itself to a much wider public. Of course, in the past, in the nineteenth century, history could partly be looked on as literature. These relationships always change. But it seems to me that there has been a change in the influence of the historian on the public. I would like some more information on this phenomenon which astonishes me.

The other point which interested me is somewhat different. Gordon Craig mentioned that the teaching of history in the United States is in decline, that people no longer know about their history and he expressed his regret – and I share it – about this development. It seems to me, however, that historians should be aware of their responsibility in this development. To assume that one can talk about, discuss and teach the history of the twentieth century more or less as a continuation of the history of previous centuries seems to me impossible. The modern world, the world which began with the development of modern capitalism and industrialism, is simply a different world and you cannot expect people who have grown up in this world to be interested in the past unless it is made very clear to them why the past is still of interest. I think that the failure to distinguish between the developments of the last sixty or eighty years and previous history is one of the reasons for the decline of interest in the past.

It seems to me that history today has to begin with the change in the position of Europe in the world and that it cannot any longer be seen from the point of view of the importance which Europe had before. If one looks at the *Historikerstreit* and the issues it raises, there is a kind of harking back to a Europe with national states, hegemony over the world, which no longer exists. It is important to adapt to the new switch which has developed in the age of the superpowers, in the Far East and in Africa and not to believe that things should be connected with the past again without being aware of the changed world situation.

SAMUEL ETTINGER: I would like first of all to say that a very important point has not been sufficiently emphasized, namely that post-war Germany did not choose democracy, democracy was imposed on Germany. The majority of Germans accepted it and adapted to Western ideas and institutions. This process was on the whole sincere on the part of most Germans after the disillusionment with Nazism, but not of all Germans. The recent trends are, in my view, due to a feeling that the decline in influence of the United States and Europe has brought about a situation where everything should be reconsidered. That is why the debate is taking place now. The economic and political strength which has been achieved by the Federal Republic in the 1980s has created the basis for the 'reconsideration' trend. I disagree with the clear-cut differences that have been drawn by some of the participants here between the attitude of neo-conservatives, liberals and social-democrats to historical problems. The idea that history until now was written from the point of view of the victors was not only, perhaps not even mainly, expressed by the neo-conservative historians but by some of the others too. In my view the *Historikerstreit* does not reflect differences in scholarly attitudes or even political affiliations, but is a reflection of the ideas and feelings of certain groups – maybe important groups – of the population in the Federal Republic who have reached the conclusion that now is the time to look at the history of the Nazi period from a different angle.

The other point which I feel has been neglected in the *Historikerstreit* is the problem of the connection between anti-semitism in the Wilhelmine and Weimar periods and the Nazi extermination of the Jews. I have already mentioned it and I want to stress it again and again. When Honecker visited Bergen-Belsen, he mentioned the victims but he didn't specifically mention the

Jews. It's not only Honecker who does this, it is typical of the whole communist attitude. Until the communists recognize this specificity of German anti-semitism it will never be possible to evaluate Nazism and its origins objectively – even from their point of view. The same applies to historians. They have analyzed innumerable problems, social, cultural, economic and political. But until they confront the problem of anti-semitism directly, the sources of anti-semitism, the continuity of anti-semitism and the specific character of anti-semitism in Germany, they will not be able to get a grip on their past. I don't only mean Nazi anti-semitism but also anti-semitism of other forms. Anti-semitism should not only be seen, as some German and other historians claim, as a general European phenomenon. It is true that there are general Christian and European origins of anti-semitism, but there is this specificity of German anti-semitism. There are literally thousands of publications about Jews in German from various points of view. Anti-semitism played an important role in the cultural development of Germany, and not to see it as one of the main points in the analysis of National Socialism is, in my opinion, a distorted approach to it.

About the connection between historical analysis and national or public consciousness, from the very beginning of the existence of nation states, history played a major role as a cohesive element, enabling a group to consider itself a nation. Maybe we are already beyond this stage and should now look for a wider, more universal concept. The fact is, however, that borders, currencies and flags still exist. People consider themselves as Czechs, or Bulgarians or whatever and as long as they do so, the common past will be one of the major elements of cohesion. On the other hand, it must be emphasized that the search for the past should not be undertaken with a particular purpose in mind. It should not for example be used to justify governmental policies as in the Soviet Union (it is called *sotsialny zakaz*, social order) where the party gives the historian a task and he fulfils it. That is not historical research, it is political falsification. Although the study of history has an extraordinary function in creating cohesion it should be objective and free of any pedagogical, moral or any other purpose. History should be studied to verify facts and trends; it should serve as a basis for possible moral judgements, political evaluations and so on. The study of history provides people with a wider experience of a culture, of a state.

Robert Conquest has spoken as though Soviet historians were

now in a state of turmoil. This situation where historical research is limited and regulated is not new, it has existed throughout Soviet history. One of the principal ways of evaluating the change brought about by Glasnost will be if the archives are opened and historians are permitted to do research freely, as has been the case in the Federal Republic of Germany.

Finally, a comment on totalitarianism. I still believe that the misuse of the term is greater than the usefulness of it. As I said, there are similarities between Stalinism and Hitlerism, but they should not be evaluated according to abstract principles, by talking about the one-party system or lawlessness. They are important, but there is a one-party system and lawlessness in states like Zaire or Uganda without totalitarianism. It is therefore essential to differentiate. Hitler and Stalin both wanted to impose their will on the population, but there was one major difference. Hitler had a perfect bureaucratic machine in his hands which had worked since the times of Frederick II. Anyone who opens the Smolensk archive, the only authentic Soviet archive we have in complete form, will see that Soviet bureaucracy was in chaos; the authorities made decisions but the ability to implement them was very limited. How can you compare this with the German form of totalitarianism? I agree that both regimes were autocratic, but again I warn against making this easy comparison between Hitlerism and Stalinism. They were two different systems, based on two different historical traditions, and trying to achieve two different political purposes.

Ralf Dahrendorf announced that he would have to restrict all further speakers to five minutes as time was running out.

NORMAN STONE: What I wanted to say has been said by Gordon Craig very splendidly. We have had a certain display of pure brotherly love among our German colleagues and I would like to join George Weidenfeld in saying that West Germany since 1945 is a tremendous success story. I go there and I feel envious. Parts of the British state, the British education system, the arts creak. I very much admire the way the German state has functioned and I think this present government in England, which is working at trying to run a centralized system, should look seriously at Germany. A great deal of the German success since 1945 has to do with the strong state. This is a central theme in German history and there are, of course, many aspects one worries about. I fully endorse what Hugh Trevor-Roper says about Germany being an appalling warning of what can go wrong with a strong state.

Leaving the Nazis aside, before 1914 you would look at Germany from the perspective of Paris or London and you would say that this was a country heading for trouble because it had no idea of a proper liberal handling of the rising Left. For instance, one country which legally, that is to say without a coup d'état, abolished universal suffrage in this century, was Saxony in 1907. It had a system approximating universal suffrage and, if I remember rightly, it substituted it with a five-class franchise, the reason for this being that the workers were rebellious, Social Democrats were getting into the diet so the Catholics made a deal with the Liberals whereby the Catholics would lose some votes in order that the Social Democrats would lose all votes.

However Germany between 1870 and 1914 is, to be fair-minded, *the* great success story of Europe. How much of that success depends on a certain kind of authoritarianism in the schools, trade unions, political opposition, is a question which should be put and I think it is interesting to look at German history in that light. In other words, the sort of thing the British and French were accusing the Germans of doing may in the end have been the cause of some success.

Since the great and good Sir Isaiah has had a go at me for saying that Russian history was not entirely tyrannical, it occurred to me that a great part of what we regard as the tyrannical side of Russia is actually an importation from, and in some ways a parody of Germany. You will be aware of the thugs lining the stairs at communist congresses holding stop watches and saying 'cut' after about fifteen minutes of exhausting applause. I stand corrected, but I think it is true to say that that habit comes from the German Social Democratic party after 1914, the reason being that the various factions of the Social Democrats had worked out that one way to silence their opponents was to applaud their own people endlessly until the opponents got bored and left the room.

I think it is worth pointing out that there is good and bad about Germany and that Britain in particular should look at the Germany since 1945 because it has been a tremendous success.

LORD WEIDENFELD: Having listened with great interest to Professor Craig and to Noel Annan, who delivered a Hans Sachsian monologue about British historians with which I wholly concur, I would like to put forward a plea to the German historian. There is an enormous job to be done and there is a *terra incognita*. It is true, as Professor Gilbert said, that in the last three, four, five, six years a great number of works of synthesis and compendiums of German history have been produced. This is a good and a bad thing, because it is done at the expense of *Geschichte in Ein-zeldarstellungen*. What makes the British bookshops so different from the German bookshop is this. If you go into any British book-shop and ask for a life of Bonnie Prince Charlie or a book on any monarch, you will not only be given one, but five or six books all published in the past few years, all on the same subject. And why do people read them? Not so much because they want to be enlightened by this or that aspect of history or philosophy, they want to read a rattling good story and historians are there to give them that story, trying to produce history *wie es eigentlich gewesen*, in good faith but with an eye on readability. That means that history is absorbed by induction. People read stories, they read about kings and queens and their foul deeds, about miscarriages of justice, of evil men and that creates a historical consciousness. By dipping into the more synthetic work of history as well, they obtain a *Wissen um die großen Zusammenhänge*, an understanding of the wider context, in a Goethian sense.

I think that is missing in Germany. It seems to me that German historians, including some of our friends here, have clout with publishers. If Christian Meier or Wolfgang Mommsen or Joachim Fest were to go to their publishers and say, I want to write about the Anabaptists, or about the phenomenon of the 'Musenhof' in Weimar, they would immediately be given a commission and thousands of Germans through book clubs and the like would learn about the splendour of Weimar, about Götz von Berlichingen and so on. This is what is needed in Germany. This would create a historical consciousness and I think therefore that there should be a historians' lobby to put pressure on the media, on the publishers for more German history according, of course, to the canons of the structure of German history which is not on the whole as monarchocentric as British history.

A brief word on Professor Ettinger's distinction between Sta-linism and Hitlerism. I think one important difference which keeps coming up is that in the family of totalitarianism, German totalitarianism is a morganatic offspring with a very uncertain provenance. It is interesting to speculate what would have hap-pened if Hitler had died in 1938 or '39. His succession was uncertain and the orientation of his successors would have been quite unpredictable. Goering would probably have lead to revisionism beyond recognition, Himmler would have done something else and the combination of Speer and Jodl would have produced different results again. Stalinism, communism had a rationalist provenance through Marx, through the filter of Lenin and, as we have seen, Stalin's death has not fundamentally changed the system. There is a provenance, there is continuity and it is going to be much more difficult to change it.

MICHAEL STÜRMER: Three points. With all due respect to Professor Ettinger, I would like to say that it is a little dangerous to persuade the Germans that democracy was imposed on them. Technically he is right as far as the first few months of 1945 are concerned. But ever since democracy has flourished and no one, not even the 'Parlamentarischer Rat', forced us to adopt the Basic Constitutional Law, let alone to continue on that path. We did that of our own free choice.

SAMUEL ETTINGER: Is it true or isn't it?

MICHAEL STÜRMER: It is not true. I have heard some Germans say exactly the same thing. It goes back to Weimar and the theory that the Republic was an alien system imposed on Germanic tribes. I don't like it and I think it is historically untrue. My second point is about history and the general public. What Lord Weidenfeld advised German historians to do, has been done by publishers. Piper Profile is, for example, an open-ended series of short essay-like biographies. Then there is DTV's Neue Deutsche Weltgeschichte or Neue Europäische Geschichte and Siedler Corso, again, a series of essays on various subjects. These books are read because there seems to be a real demand for them. As to the more substantial point raised by Professor Gilbert. The books he saw in the bookshops are not subsidized. They are made for commercial profit. DVA's history of the Federal Republic is, as Eberhard Jäckel knows better than I, a commercial success.

RALF DAHRENDORF: Would it not be true to say that the research that has gone into these books is likely to be subsidized and that quite a lot of money is available for this kind of research?

MICHAEL STÜRMER: That's quite right, research can be subsidized through the *Deutsche Forschungsgemeinschaft*, directly or indirectly, and universities are basically there for the same reason. But there has been a tremendous change, these books were not available ten years ago. Why is this? I think the sixties were a time when sociology and political science flourished and when economists offered their vision of the world. Now, with the decline of progress which has already been identified here, a number of questions have arisen and, strangely enough, historians and particularly economic historians, historians of political ideas are called upon to explain what is basically their stock in trade, that is to say, the Past. People expect these historians to govern some clue of what might be determining forces of the future. We historians are being invited to talk about the history of energy, we are called upon to talk about nuclear history – for obvious reasons. With the loss of certainty about the future there is a growing tendency to ask questions that look for certainty in the past. There is also a tendency to ask theological questions, but that is a different matter.

All the questions that tend to come up in this way have surprisingly little to do with the issues raised by the *Historikerstreit*. People are concerned with international politics, energy, nuclear problems, security, arms control, confidence building, with where the Soviet Union and the United States are going, with how one could effect a transformation from the bipolar system to a multi-polar system in which Europe can perhaps have a role, they are concerned with how to effect the transition from smoke-stack industries to more modern industries, with the role of Germany and that of France, the role of women, the way of life and the way of death. These are the questions that are implicitly or explicitly asked and there is an astonishing demand for comments from historians. Often, of course, they are so set in their ways that they never feel provoked by these questions. But it is healthy even for the most orthodox angry young men of the sixties, when old age is approaching, to be challenged in this way. I think these developments have not so much changed the way historians perceive themselves, but rather the perception the public has of what history is about and what historians have to offer.

CHARLES MAIER: Despite what Michael Stürmer has said, I think there is a link with the *Historikerstreit* and I would like to comment on it. Ralf Dahrendorf posed three questions: why was this particular conflict so bitter; why have analogous conflicts come up in other countries; and why now? As I have already indicated, I think America has seen an equivalent reaching out for an experiential history. The attempt at coming to terms with Vietnam, at accepting the veterans, at revalorizing the combat experience while not losing a critical stance towards the war has, in a sense, been analogous to what has been going on in Germany and in Japan. The most successful *Mahnmal* of all is our Vietnamese memorial. It is immensely touching, it moves even those of us who were opposed to the war and it works well because it is spontaneous, it is not manipulated.

I think the question of 'why now?' boils down to the role of history. Wolfgang Mommsen gave a very good summary. Essentially we have seen the breakdown of what one might call a social science paradigm in stages since 1968. Wolfgang Mommsen called it neo-liberal, I think of it as more Keynesian or social democratic. It presupposed that there were really no insuperable conflicts in industrial society. It had an agenda – one would pass from the political control of men to the administration of things. It was a paradigm free of conflict and there was a whole sociological industry and ideology attached to it. It is no accident that post-war Germany and post-war Japan were creations of that era. It was to a certain degree a German sociology taken to the United States and elsewhere, purged of its earlier decisionist conflictual elements and reimported into Germany. It broke down and it broke down from both political directions. I think Wolfgang Mommsen is right in saying that that breakdown effected a return to history, a return to hermeneutics and a more subjective protocol. This is what Habermas, I think rightly, fears because he is affected by it. He was himself a left-wing variant of that particular ideology. He believes in evolution, in modernism, he has felt threatened by neo-Nietzschian neo-romanticism since the early seventies. The old paradigm having broken down, I think the history one must return to is a history that presupposed conflictuality. The former paradigm presupposed harmony and I believe it was exceptional. I do not think it could have lasted, it was the product of certain post-war conditions.

As we return to history, historians must be prepared to live with conflict. It is no accident, though in a sense I regret it, that Nietzsche and Carl Schmitt are back in favour. I always linger with the sentence from Thucydides, who is after all the father of our profession – Professor Craig mentioned it indirectly – and that is that the strong do what they will and the weak do what they must. This is the world that historians are being called upon to deal with. The essence of politics is conflict of will. But, although I do not mean to be Schmittian, let me suggest that conflict does not mean that every conflict is a concealed war. There are two modes of recognizing that conflictuality and conflictuality for historical orientation exist. Norman Gash cites Melbourne as saying in the late 1830s, that the fault of the present time is that men hate each other so damnably. But within a decade that type of conflict had been channelled into political routine, search for office turned into party politics. This is what happened in America in the 1970s, it is what happened in my faculty in the few years from 1968 until 1974, when you had conservatives and liberal caucuses instead of policemen versus students.

There is a Hobbesian model of conflictuality which I sometimes fear will be resorted to and there is a Groosian model of conflictuality where there are still rules of intercourse, where people disagree but people can sit at a table and dine with one another. History can be a Groosian enterprise with rules of the game that do not eliminate conflict but make it possible for it not to end in civil war. Those rules relate to the use of evidence for example. Of all the participants in this *Historikerstreit* the only one who I can see myself being forced into non-commonality by, as Saul Friedlander was, is not here. I certainly disagree with other interpretations of German history but that doesn't preclude discussing them, indeed, it is important to do so. History is the discipline which is chosen to deal with a world of many orientations and universes, so we as historians should be particularly adept at interpreting the current political world. In this sense I think that the *Historikerstreit* does relate to whether we engage in history of the international system, or energy, or whatever. It should teach us how to do our craft.

CHRISTIAN MEIER: I see certain problems with regard to the production of historical books. On the one hand we have behind us a long period of what I would call the withdrawal of historians from the public, where we more or less entrenched ourselves in the ramparts of our professions. At the same time we have a break which is not untypical of German historical science. It has been brought about by the fact that we are questioning many conventions, not least the customary way of writing history, and we are now finding it difficult to revive that traditional historiography which used, after all, to be so magnificent in Germany. One could make a virtue of this break by thinking anew about how history should be written and by deliberately including in these deliberations problems which arise because history, with its anthropological dimension, everyday history and the like, has now become more than it was. We should not, in my opinion, go about it by lining up all these things side by side. Instead we must work out thorough syntheses for creating a history of our century, and by that I do not mean a history which deals with our century but one that is worthy of it.

On the other hand there is a problem of receptivity. I would say that Felix Gilbert's question can largely be answered by the fact that for a long time there was a dearth of historical representations and that now there is a certain demand for them. The historians were not aware of it at first, a few publishers recognized it in time. In fact some, like Wolf Jobst Siedler, have always tried to cater for historical interests with such works as Joachim Fest's *Hitler* and Golo Mann's *Wallenstein* and they have been very successful. But it took some time for it to become apparent that there was such a strong demand and historians were more or less taken by surprise. The difference can easily be seen by comparing today's bookshops with the endless amount of sociological, pedagogical, didactic literature that would have filled the shelves around 1972. Today such publications take up very little space. An important leftist-orientated publisher in Germany told me the other day that he had recently thrown all these books away, they were not even good enough for it to be worth giving them to a second hand bookshop, there was nothing left but to throw them into the dustbin.

Having got rid of that wave, and, after all, intellectual life does go in waves, the new wave is history. There is another factor and that is that Germans, who seem to have discovered tourism as a great historical mission, now know most foreign countries including places like Bali and Thailand so that the only thing which is still foreign to them is their own history. That is travelling in time. This does not exclude what Herr Stürmer was saying; of course people are interested in modern issues like history of energy and international relations. But the real interest is, in my view, a history of a voyage in time. There is no other way of explaining why the Middle Ages have experienced such a boom, which has only been catered for by French publications so far and all we can do is translate them. The more exotic the subject, the better, as though interest in such things were proof of exoticism.

The question now is: how should historians respond with regard to their literary output as well as to the teaching of history in schools and so on? I think students find it particularly difficult to understand political history today, Gordon Craig addressed himself to this. Everyday history doesn't pose a problem, however exotic it may be, neither do sociological structures, at least if they are presented in a way that is easily grasped by the lay mind. But accessibility to politics-in-the-making is extremely difficult, and I wonder if it is at all possible to put across political history to young people unless they in some way identify with the state and political order. We can only revitalize political history if we start on a lower level, that is to say anthropolitically, on a level where everybody is affected by politics, where the student is made to understand why there must be a body politic. Political history can only ever be part of history, it must be incorporated into a wider context. That requires a great deal of work, it cannot be done on the side with a few small articles, it requires patience and it means that the teaching of history in schools, if it is to be revived, must be done under different auspices. The old way of teaching history continued in the tradition of the nineteenth century. This is now a thing of the past. The new way of teaching history must, in my view, be orientated towards conflict since teachers have different political perspectives, different approaches and they will look at history from their point of view. We cannot expect easy solutions in instilling new life into the teaching of history, but we will have to put to the test those qualities which were lacking in the *Historikerstreit*.

LORD DACRE: We have moved away from the details of the *Historikerstreit* and have got onto another level which seems to be much more suitable for the end of a conference like this. In my opinion, historians don't and shouldn't determine policy. They should comment on policy, they should correct historical errors which are used to justify political actions and false analogies which can be so disastrous in action. It is of course true that historical traditions built up by historians can have a political force which can be put behind particular programmes. Wolfgang Mommsen has given some examples. In his book on Macaulay, John Clive describes how Macaulay's great speech on the English Reform Bill of 1832 had its enormous effect because he was able to put behind that programme the weight of a historical tradition, the Whig tradition, of which he was the new interpreter. This gave a new dimension and a new force to that particular programme, and indeed to the English political party which advocated it, for the rest of that century.

In the same century we have evidence of such a political force in the German historians who were so influential in bringing about a consensus in support of the Bismarckian Empire. The tradition which they created was powerful enough to survive the defeat of 1918. But then Ranke and Meinecke were overtaken by another great 'universal historian', Adolf Hitler. He too believed that he had an understanding of history and indeed he had read a great deal and thought a great deal about it, and he fitted all this into a system which was internally coherent and recognizably a continuation, but also a perversion, of the nineteenth century political philosophy. Professor Jäckel has brought that out in his book on Hitler's *Weltanschauung*.

Any historian is likely to be found wrong, particularly 150 years after he has written, but basically I think that Macaulay's interpretation of English history can be defended and is more defensible than the alternatives that have been put up against it. But the German historical tradition of the nineteenth century was unsatisfactory, and that Hitler's perversion of it was politically disastrous. Altogether, I think that the dangers of allowing historians to build up historical traditions useful in politics are greater than the advantages. The necessary corrective is a continuing heretical tradition. That means open debate and constant criticism such as does not exist in totalitarian societies.

My hero in the nineteenth century is Jacob Burckhardt who escaped from the consensus of the German historians to Switzerland and was a lone dissentient voice throughout the latter part of the century. It is, I think, a very moving moment in the biography of Friedrich Meinecke when, at the end of his very long life, he said in his inaugural speech at the Free University of Berlin that perhaps in the end we would have to admit that not Ranke, who had been the polar star of his career, but Burckhardt had been right. The lesson is, I think, that the function of historians does not lie in building and maintaining historical traditions to be used in politics, far less in defending particular political decisions or episodes. Historians must be critical. They must be professional, they must correct errors of other historians – which they do very willingly – and of course of politicians. But they also have a positive function which is more general than that. It is to teach history objectively and, by discussion, to enable a general historical wisdom to emerge which is not applicable only to the particular issues under discussion but should serve to put the present in the context of the past and enable politicians to think clearly on important political matters and perhaps thereby prevent serious errors.

JOACHIM FEST: Much of what I was going to say in conclusion has been dealt with by the speakers who preceded me. On the whole, despite the differences that have emerged here, I believe we are agreed that history, the image we create for it and that we put across, is extremely important.

Regarding the difficulties of communication which were referred to earlier, I would like to mention an attempt made by Christian Meier and myself at bridging the gap between historians and the public. We planned to publish a series in the *Frankfurter Allgemeine* called 'Erzählte Geschichte', narrated history. The correspondence dealing with this project fills several files. But all that came out of it were three contributions that were fit to be printed. All the others had to be sent back to those authors who had at least agreed to take part in the project. Many historians did not even do that. We can't boast such an impressive list as the one reeled off by Lord Annan when he spoke about British history writing. Christian Meier remarked that the demand for history did not surface until very late in Germany. I must contradict him on that point. Not only was the need for it not recognized so that we cannot say whether it was there or not, but even if it was not there, it could have been roused, and none other than the historians should have seen it as their task to do so.

They should look back to the German nineteenth century tradition of history, even though I agree with what Lord Dacre said about its disastrous influence. But one could mention Mommsen's *Römische Geschichte*, which was written for a large public as a counter example. One can also think of Jacob Burckhardt who consciously turned his back on academic ivory towers and always took the needs of the public into account. His statements on this subject provide food for thought. I would also like to give a contemporary example. A few years ago Karl Dietrich Bracher wrote a comprehensive book on the Third Reich called *Die Deutsche Diktatur*. I know from conversations with him that he had many scruples about it. He once said how difficult it is to write a book without footnotes. We all feel like that and sometimes I have the impression that the works of German historians are written with the sole purpose of publishing significant footnotes garnished with a few lines of text.

Lord Dacre has said that historians should not want to have political influence. I agree wholeheartedly and it is unfortunate that we have lost sight of the subject which indirectly pervaded our discussion. Thomas Mann once said that the novelist should not want to have a moral influence. Instead he should put all his effort into writing a good novel with a strong story and convincing characterizations. If he succeeds, the work will of itself have moral influence. The same applies to the writing of history. It should not pursue political aims. But if it awakes interest in the past and can depict the people who participated in it convincingly, it will also have the political influence which must be important to us, despite all the differences.

CAROL GLUCK: I appreciate what Christian Meier said about opportunities that this kind of consideration of history offers. I was struck by four points and, at risk of sounding optimistic – a risk I'm willing to take – I also see four opportunities. There is an opportunity in the disintegration of the models we have spoken about. The questioned authority of the social sciences and the vitiated claim to scientific validity are disintegrative forces, but they also offer an opportunity for conceptual creativity.

There is an old Chinese story about some helpful characters who went to assist Chaos because he was ailing. On the first day the wizard drilled a hole in Chaos, and Chaos still felt ill. On the second day he drilled a second hole to help the vapours escape and the third a third. On the fourth day he drilled a fourth hole and on the fifth a fifth hole. And Chaos died. This ministration to Chaos may offer us an analogy: Chaos may die and the crisis of intellectual authority may be an opportunity for creative political social thought, which we surely need.

Second, all that has been said about the woeful state of historical instruction is more or less true of many countries. Rather than concentrate solely on education in the schools we should perhaps be equally concerned with mass historical consciousness. Historians need not be confined to writing books for a lay public, but they might follow the Japanese example where historians are media stars who appear on television and write about history for the weekly magazines. If we are talking about mass historical consciousness which translates into political consciousness then by all means we should use the media to which we are all heir. They offer a grand opportunity for education

Third, I think the *Historikerstreit* gives us an opportunity to move from what has been contested here and from name-calling and polemic to the searching reflection of what Wolfgang Mommsen called 'perspectives'. There are perspectives embedded in all of our history-writing, and it would be wise if we worked more to identify them. This is a political opportunity since we all express our politics in our history-writing. Looking at the Soviet Union, or China, where the writing of history is determined by politics, we in freer societies feel that this is not the correct condition for history and imagine we are exempt from these political perspectives. This dispute offers us an opportunity to clarify our own positions. They are likely to be more complicated than we may have thought. This complexity has emerged in the course of the conference and offers us an opportunity for reflection on our personal politics as well.

Fourth, I think there is an opportunity to move from the concentration on national identity to a cognizance of international context, to move away from Germano-centrism or Japano-centrism – the same applies to other countries like China, which still thinks of itself as the Central Kingdom – and to use this re-evaluation of history to assert and reassert the international context as well as the national one. I would like to cite another passage from Thucydides, where he remarks that rewriting history is essentially a case of people adapting their memories to suit their suffering. I think we should acknowledge that each of these nations has its own sufferings and that it needs to adapt its memory to them. It should not, however, be done at the expense of the suffering of other nations or at the expense of seeing one's sufferings in the context of other nations. This re-evaluation therefore presents an opportunity for world politics, for international relations, if only we escape from the confines of entirely national history.

These four points comprise what someone once called a range of insurmountable opportunities for the historian of the present who wishes to keep his eye on the potential relationship between politics and history.

JÜRGEN KOCKA: I would also like to take up one of Felix Gilbert's questions and say something about the meaning and the dangers of this growing interest in history. I don't believe there was a loss of history in the sixties and early seventies, as is sometimes said. The protest movements of the time liked to argue in historical terms, though perhaps in a different way from today. Important developments within the historical profession took place in that period, the rise of social history is an example. Nonetheless, interest in history has increased markedly in the last ten or fifteen years. This is reflected in the book trade, in the public exposure given to historians, in the *Historikerstreit* where fundamental problems concerning the Federal Republic were discussed through the medium of history. One should stress that the general public is not only showing a greater interest in national history but in local and regional history as well. In Germany as in other countries there is a movement of *Geschichtswerkstätten*, history workshops, and *Heimatgeschichte*, local history, is enjoying a boom. So the new interest in history isn't necessarily a movement towards national history.

Many reasons have been given for the recent growth of interest in history. I would like to suggest another explanation. In the sixties there was a widespread feeling that everything was too stable, too rigid, and many intellectuals, reformers and protesters saw it as their task to set something in motion. At some point in the seventies this mood changed; now there is a widespread feeling that we are living in a time where things are moving too fast and that they can't be controlled any more. It is in this mood that history has been rediscovered, that there is a new demand for history. History is required as a stabilizing factor or as a form of escape from the rapidly changing world.

I have simplified the argument, but if it is correct it means that the conservatory functions of history are now being stressed, whereas in the sixties and seventies one tended to speak more about the critical functions of history. I don't dispute that history can have conservatory functions, but there are two problems involved. Firstly, I agree with Lord Dacre; we should insist that history also has its critical functions. History should be critical about legends but in a more general sense it should be used to show that present matters which seem self-evident are not all that self-evident. History opens up choices. It also provides tools with which to analyse the present. We should not lose sight of these critical functions.

Secondly, although historians usually welcome the interest publishers and journalists express in their work, we must not forget that we are a profession, and that the expectations of the public alone cannot guide our work. It isn't entirely wrong that we should want to be quoted, and quoted accurately by other historians, that we should want to be taken seriously by our colleagues and not just by the general public. Incidentally, in this professional context footnotes are important. Furthermore, it is more difficult to write books with footnotes than without them. Historians must preserve a certain professional autonomy. We have had quite a number of synthetical works now, perhaps there are even some repetitive elements in this business of writing synthetical history books at the moment. But these works build on specialized research. Specialized work is central to the profession, whether journalists find it boring or not. Professional identity may provide us with a weapon with which to resist certain instrumentalizations of history. It is normal that there should be a gap between the population at large and the historical profession. Historians should not pretend to be journalists.

RALF DAHRENDORF: I am particularly grateful for Jürgen Kocka's rehabilitation of the footnote because I was going to describe the latter part of this conference as 'Thoughtful footnotes on an important debate'. It is perhaps an appropriate way of summing up what happened here. History matters, whether one likes it or not, historians have a wide audience and history also reflects currents in the public mood in a significant way.